Chesapeake Bay Karma

Book One: The Amulet

JM Johansen and Narielle Living

High Tide Publications
HARDYVILLE, VIRGINIA

High Tide Publications
Post Office Box 183
Hardyville, Virginia 23070
www.HighTidePublications.com

Publisher's Note: This is a work of fiction. Names, characters, places, and incidents are a product of the authors' imaginations. Locales and public names are sometimes used for atmospheric purposes. Any resemblance to actual people, living or dead, or to businesses, companies, events, institutions, or locales is completely coincidental.

Cover Design: Matthew Archambault and Carl Johansen

Chesapeake Bay Karma/JM Johansen and Narielle Living -- 1st Edition
ISBN 978-0988463752

Dedication

This book is dedicated to the women in our lives who paved the way for us, who spoke for those who had no voice because they were afraid, who showed us by their example that silence would not save us.

Book I

Josie

Josie

People always think that a little bit of magic can make anything better. But when it comes to fixing a broken spirit, no amount of magic can right that kind of wrong.

I spent the first part of my childhood sitting on the shore listenin' to the waves lick the sand for long periods of time. Sometimes the moon was big, round, and full, and sometimes it stayed shrouded in the soft black of the sky once the sun was done with its day's journey. I will never forget that hot, sticky morning when I was about ten years old. It was the morning my world changed forever. There was a sliver of a moon over the water as the sun rose behind my back. The water sparkled with the beginning light and the sky turned a pale shade of dark. So quiet, and yet I had this feelin' it was all 'bout to change.

Round the point that morning came a form. It was a sea creature, one that I had heard 'bout from the old people in my village. It had three spears stickin' outta it's side and a long snake-tongue jabbing straight out ahead of it. It stopped out in the water and sat there. I could hear voices, like the people the monster ate were still alive in its belly. It musta been dead 'cause it didn't move.

I ran home an got my mama and told her 'bout the monster. I pulled her by her left arm and we hid in the bush.

She look out to the sea and started breathin' real fast, and then she fell back. "That ain't no sea monster," she whispered. "That be a slave ship."

I had been warned my whole life about the ships that came to our shores. Sure enough, it happened just like they said it would. As the sky grew lighter with daybreak, men came off the big boat, and got rowed to shore in smaller boats. They threw out bright pieces of cloth on the sandy beaches of my homeland, tiny pieces of colors I had never seen. The color of the red birds in the trees. The color of the sky. They came down, fluttering and waving on the sand.

"You never touch those things," Mama whispered. "No matter what, you never touch. The men who throw them, they will run and grab you and carry you off."

Mama dragged me back home, away from those ships. Save me from the slavers.

This mornin' I heard a commotion in my village. There was a big boat in the harbor again. I ran with my friends, and I saw them pull up to the shore in their little boats. I stayed far back. Up in the tree I stayed and never came down, not 'til those men had gone back to the big ship out in the water. They came on the first day with little things. The others ran out and picked them up and took them things home to their huts back in the bush. Not me. I stayed in that tree.

The next day I went back to the beach, watching. They came again, this time with all sorts of pretty bright things and they threw them on the sand. This time more people came out from the bush and they picked these new presents up and took them with them.

Then the third day the silver men came ashore with trunks, and they opened them up on the sand of my beaches and they waited for the others to come. The trunks have bright and shiny things and the people, they came. The men from the big ship, they grabbed the younger men and women and they tied their hands and feet and dragged them back to the boat that brought them to the big ship. I watched it all from my hiding place up in that tree.

The people from the bush, they ran after the small boat screaming and yelling for those men to bring back their sons, brothers, daughters, sisters. But the boat was too fast and they watched with me as the men pulled the people of my village onto the big boat. Some of my people, they died in the water going out, and them men from the big ship just tossed them back into the ocean.

Later their bodies come up on the beach like the colored cloth and shiny things the men threw on the beach. I ran home and told my mama what had happened. She whipped me good 'cause I was even there.

Now, my mama was a conjurer. She made gris-gris for our neighbors. People, they come from all around to our little hut for the charms and prayers. She was a powerful woman, my mama. She helped so many people. And the ones that needed to be done away with, well she would give them the disease to kill them off if need be. Some people, they call my mama a witch but she weren't no witch. No sir! She was a healer, and sometime you gotta get rid of people to heal your life.

I couldn't stop thinkin' bout slave ships and bodies on the beach.

So, I stopped sleepin' at night and I stopped eatin' at daytime, and by the end of the third day I was pretty sick. So mama, she made me a gris-gris of my own. She had the skin of a bongo that one of the hunters from our village had killed. She cut the belly skin and wrote special prayer symbols on the skin before she made me a little pouch from it. "It is protection from the fire," she said. "I will teach you when I finish."

My mama, she worked on that gris-gris for three days and three nights. She put a special stone on a cord inside, along with some bones, and then she made me a luck ball with a special cord on it made from cat gut. She put the luck ball in there, too. She finished it off with a cord so I could hang it from my neck or 'round my waist.

That night, mama said to get myself ready. She was takin' me to a special place and she was gonna give me my gris-gris. There was a full moon, and it lit up the sky and you could see very little of the stars 'cause the ol moon was so bright. We went to a clearin' just past our village. The trees kinda leaned into each other and made a little hut, all those leaves growin' together at the top.

There was this pile of brush in the middle, and when my mama took it away I saw a pile of stones with a piece of wood on top. It was the strangest table I ever did see! I remember there were all kinds of carvings in the wood, carvings of women and symbols and things I'd never seen before. My mama put the candle on top of the board that made this table. She opened the pouch, and took everything out of the bag and put them next to the candle too. There were nine things in there, and she sprinkled each of them with the water she carried in a little bottle in the pouch 'round her waist.. She fastened a little doll that looked just like me to the front of the pouch. The doll's hair was made from hair from my very own head.

Mama put all the little things back 'cept the luck ball. She put it 'round my neck first, and slung it over my left shoulder and over my right side so it was right under my armpit. "It must stay against your naked body so you get all it's strength," she said. Then she put the pouch round my neck. "I'm gonna teach you sometin' now, but you must forever keep it to yourself," she said as she put her hand on my shoulders.

I heard men shouting from the direction of our village, and saw the light from their torches filtering through the canopy of the trees. "We need to run, mama. They comin' for us."

"Quiet, child," she whispered as she drew a circle in the dirt, walking 'round to the left. When she was finished, she stepped inside and bid me follow her. We walked three times around the inside of the circle to the left. Then she taught me to say these three prayers which I ain't gonna write down 'cause she said to never tell no one and I ain't gonna start disobeyin' my mama now. Even though she be dead for many a year, I still feel her sometimes.

"Now sit in the center of the circle," she said. I did like she said and all of a sudden we was both under the ground in this big place. There was other women there, some who I knowed had died long ago. They greeted my mama, hugging and holdin' her. "This is my daughter, who tonight joined our sisterhood," she said. "Tonight she becomes one of us."

All that night they prayed over me, one by one. I slept for the first time in days and ate the food they gave me. We laughed and sang songs and by morning I felt like I was brand new.

My mama, she taught me what to say to go back above ground. "As long as you be in the circle I showed you and you got your gris-gris, you safe. No one can harm you, but you gots to stay in the circle. Remember that. And this necklet that I put round your neck last night, as long as you got that on no one can burn you with fire. They gonna try, but it will protect you from the flames. Make sure now you keep that luck ball under your arm like I showed you, next to your skin, so you stay safe."

We walked back to the village in the warm morning sun. The path wandered here and there, and had been made that way so we could run into the bush if enemies attacked. When we rounded the last bend we saw our village, burned to the ground and not another human insight.

I swallowed back my tears, knowing they wouldn't help now. No good cryin' over evil, you just got to get away.

Mama turned to me. "We got to go back and find another village, see if any of our people survived."

"Can't we jus' go back and stay with the sisters under the ground?" I asked. I was terrified.

"No, honey. That's the spirit world down there. It will be our home someday, but not now. We gotta find another place up here to stay safe."

And so, we started walking We came upon the altar and the circle from last night. .It had been burned right to the ground. Some of the trees had strange markings on them. Mama turned to me. "They got a conjurer with them. Don' touch them trees. See those herbs and powder? It may be an evil one did that, cast a powerful spell where we walked last."

"Can you stop the power, Mama?" I knew she was a root doctor who could give us safety and stop whatever curse was there.

"Yes, child. But I have nothing with me to put a potion together. Everything was burned when…"

We heard rustling in the leaves above us. "It's the wind," I thought. "Has to be just the wind."

Mama musta heard it too 'cause she looked up. "Jus' the wind," she said in a reassuring voice.

We started to walk around the trees where she drew the circle last night. More rustlin', this time from the bushes that lined the path on both sides.

Mama stopped and drew a circle in the path and walked three times to her left just like last night. "Get in the circle, and walk three times to the left like you just saw me do," she whispered. "Do not, no matter what you see or hear, leave that circle. You are safe as long as you stay protected in that circle. Do you understand?"

I nodded, walked three times to the left completely around the inside of the circle, and sat in the middle.

"I love you, child."

"I love you, mama."

She raised her arms above her head and started rockin' back and forth. She took her luck ball outta her bodice and started swinging it 'round above her head. "Oh spirits afore me, spirits behind me, spirits be with me. Strike down the devils that wish us harm. Tie down all devils, bind my enemies before me and bring them under my feet. I ask for your protection, mighty spirit. Drive these men from us. Save us from harm. Save us."

Then mama started chantin' and wailin' and jumpin' up an down. She was scarin' me and she was my mama!

Suddenly, from the tree above us, three men fell to the ground and started rolling 'round in the dirt and screamin' in pain. The louder they scream the louder mama scream. Then this man with a club, he run out the bushes and he screamin' and heading for mama. He had the eyes of a snake with a big, flat forehead above them. His nose had flaring nostrils and it look like there was hot steam pourin' outta them. He looked like the devil himself. He pulled a spear behind him and headed straight for mama. His big lips were pulled back to show a double row of brown and yellow, broken teeth separated by a wriggling snake tongue. He headed straight for my mama, but I sat still, obedient to her warning. He ran right through me as if I was not there.

The devil himself stopped short of grabbing mama when he saw the three other men lying dead on the ground at his feet. He turned to the man that had been hiding with him in the bush and saw that he, too, had fallen on the ground in a terrible state of pain. Sensing there was no one to back him, he escaped down the path to whatever destination awaited him.

When mama saw he had run off she stopped her wailin' and screamin' and walked over to the circle where I sat, my eyes as big as the moon last night.

"Come, child. Let us find us a new home."

I wanna tell you that we found a safe place, a new village that welcomed us. I wanna tell you that we walked to it right away and we was happy ever after. I wanna tell you that but it ain't the way it happened.

It was the beginnin' of a bad time for us. We lost it all when they burned our village, and so my mama had no roots to use in her conjurin' and she lost her powers. We were turned away from every village when they learned my mama was a root woman. Plus, I think those stories about the men fallin' outta those trees spread like fire. But what did I know? I was just a young girl starting to come into my womanhood.

We had been travelin' for nigh on to two years when finally my mama jus' gave up and decided we would live in the bush. We built us a home in the side of a dirt mound. It had been the lair of some animal and it worked out perfect 'cause we was well hidden. I learned how to catch and skin animals. She started to gather her roots again, and pretty soon it was just our little space hidden away.

We'd been here a year or so. It was nice and I was happy again. There weren't no people or other young ones to play with, but there weren't no one trying to kill us, neither. Just me and mama.

She started teachin' me the old ways. "Use your power for good," she'd say to me. "You can heals people or hurts people. Better to make 'em better." She taught me 'bout the possum bones and how to use 'em for divination.

I started to bleed that year. Mama told me I was now a full woman, and I was sacred and full of power. She also told me 'bout men wanted to do things to me 'cause I was a woman, and how it could make a baby. She said I could conjure now and she would teach me the ancient ways to heal. At night I would have dreams 'bout things to come.

Mama gave me the necklet she wore round her neck. "Take this. It is holy, and my mama gave it to me and her mama to her, and so on and so on. It will keep you safe. The people who mean you harm will not see it round your neck. The ones who mean to help you in this life will be able to see it 'round your neck. That's how you know who is your friend and who is your enemy." Then she said a little prayer over me and when she was done I felt right powerful!

I realized my gift was with the divination and the bones. I loved those things. I would draw a circle in the dirt and put the animal skin mama had prepared in the middle. Then I would throw the bones. In the beginning it was just yes or no questions. After a time I got more and more brave. I asked 'bout my future, would I ever find a man to love like mama loved my daddy? Would I have babies and be happy?

The bones said yes. What I forgot to ask was how long it would take for that to come to pass.

1797

O utside our little cave I heard a rustling in the woods. First thing that entered my mind was a snake or somethin' like that.

It was a snake – just not the kind that crawls on its belly.

Mama musta had a foretellin' 'cause every day she made me practice the circle. I could do it faster and faster. She made me keep the necklet on, the luck ball under my armpit and my gris-gris with me at all times.

That day – the day everything changed - mama had stayed back at our little cave to clean some skins. I was wanderin' back real slow 'cause I didn't like that part. It stunk and took too long for a sixteen year old girl who was looking for exploits. Mama wouldn't let me too far from the cave for fear somethin' bad would happen.

Like I said, a foretellin'.

There was more rustling in the bush, and it had to be some big animal 'cause of all the noise it made. I stopped and squatted down and tried to see what was making all that commotion.

I heard voices coming from the brush. I didn't make no sense of what they was saying – it was just babble. I knew it was men 'cause their talk was deep. I knew they had found us.

I started to run. Sweat from the fear and the heat was drippin' in my eyes and I could feel my feet tearing on the rock. I didn't pay no mind to it; I just ran to warn mama.

Then I heard a scream, the one she used to warn me when something nasty was headed toward us. It meant she was in big danger, and it made me run even harder.

I got to the spot just before the clearin' in front of the cave. A man held her by her hair and two other men were holdin' her arms.

"Are you here alone?" I heard him ask.

Mama nodded as best she could 'cause he was holding her hair straight up and he was a whole lot taller than her.

"Then why you got two beds in that cave?" he asked.

Mama said nothing.

The spot where I was watchin' from in the woods had a little cleared space. It was big 'nuf for a circle and I drew one, walking three times inside to the left like she taught me. I sat in the middle like she had made me promise if we got trouble around us. "No matter what," she would say to me, "promise you will stay there."

The men started walking toward me, beating the bushes with sticks. They walked all 'round where I sat but they never saw me sittin' there.

"You're a witch and a conjurer and you know what awaits you."

Again, mama said nothin'.

He reached into his robe and pulled out a knife, and in one movement slit her throat. She made no sound or movement to stop him, and fell to the ground.

I screamed.

"Hear that?" one of the men said.

"It's her spirit comin' to get us," another yelled.

"Cut her apart and spread her parts all over this area. We'll take her heart back with us and burn it."

And so I watched as he cut her heart from her body and the other men hacked her arms and legs, some of which they burned right there.

I was captured not long after that. I jus' couldn't fight no more. They put me on a ship with the others and we set sail.

1800

When I was taken to the ship three years ago, I saw black people of every size and shape chained together. Children separated from their mamas. Nothin' but sadness.

Like I said, I just gave up after mama was killed, and thought nothin' was worse than that. But then I saw what was on that ship and I was overcome with horror.

I was wailin' and cryin' and carrying on, and then I stopped long enough to watch the black people who brought me aboard receiving their pay. I watched them leave the ship, and knew I would never again see my homeland.

Just afore we set sail, we was put below and the smell that hit my nostrils was the worst imaginable. I could eat nothing, instead giving my food to the others held captive. We kept silent about this 'cause we would be tied and beaten if the white men learned we refused eatables.

I prayed for Death, to be with the sisterhood below the earth, to see my mama again.

Some of the men escaped their chains and jumped over the side. Amongst the men chained below I found some of my own nationals. I asked them what was our fate, and they said we were going to the white people's land to work. At least it was workin', which made me able to sleep and on occasion eat a bit.

It been three years since I got off that terrible ship and was sold to a family in Williamsburg, Virginia. Mama warned me 'bout men and them being all sexed up, and she was right. The first days I was there my owner decided I should mate with his prized slave and have children. I bore two in the next three years. The first died right after she was born. I was glad, 'cause I never want to bring no child into this kind of life.

My owner's wife had a baby boy name of Albert. Her milk done dried up, so I was brought up to the big house to be his nurse maid. I loved that little boy and he loved me. The family, they saw that 'cause he cried when anyone but me held him. So they made me his nurse.

As he started to grow, I tried to teach him right from wrong. I knew he was a sweet boy, but that family of his let him get away with acting any which way he wanted. I caught him with an old cat one day, back out behind the barn. He was sitting in the dirt, with one of the old kitchen knives in his hand.

"Albert, what you doin' to that poor creature?" I shrieked.

His six year old eyes looked up at me, amused I would be upset. "It's only a cat, Josie."

"You can't cut up a living creature like that," I told him, taking the knife from his hands.

"I wanted to see if it screamed," he said.

I put that scene right outta my mind, because I didn't like thinking about my little boy actin' strange like that. One minute he was my sweet angel child, but the next… well, I had to stop those images or I wouldn't be able to sleep at night.

Really, they needed to stop letting that boy do whatever he wanted.

I got the sickness in October . I couldn't stay with little Albert. He was seven years now, and starting to show signs of the man he would become. I never caught him back behind the barn again, but I had a feeling he still did things I wouldn't approve of. But I admit, I loved that child like he was my own – yes I did.

On that terrible night in October, another one of the slaves stayed with Albert. It was early evening when she tipped the lantern over in his room. I heard the chants coming from the big house. "Fire, fire, fire!"

I jumped up from my sick bed and ran to the main house. 'It's Albert's room," one of the field hands yelled.

Running into the house, I pulled my luck ball from under my arm and the necklet off my neck. Albert's screams tore through me, pulling me through the thick smoke. When I finally reached him, I put everything around his neck. It was powerful hot in that room, and I could barely breathe as my clothes burned, melting onto my body.

I crawled on the floor to stay under the smoke, dragging Albert along with me. It was like the fire parted for us – just like that Moses story the missionaries told us. And I got out to the front porch and handed Albert to his daddy, and there weren't a burn on him.

I was burned to a crisp and they really thought I wouldn't live past the night. But I did, and I got better, but I had bad scars all over my body to remind me of that night.

Now, the overseer wanted to trade me off 'cause I was of no use to them as a burned up nigger. But Mr. Hutchins, he and his missus would not hear of it. So, they built me a little cabin where I could grow my roots and live out my days. I got my amulet and luck ball with me and I never takes 'em off 'cause I am scared near to death around any fire. I won't even cook on one, so the women up the main house they bring me my food. They don't like it, neither.

The other field hands they wouldn't come near me 'cause I was so scarred up. But Albert, he wasn't afraid, and we spent many happy hours together.

I love that boy!

1807

Albert

There is one person in this whole world that believes I am good, and that is my slave, Josie. Supposedly she saved me from a fire when I was but a child, but I know the truth.

The fire could not touch me.

I know the truth of who I am and what I am destined for. I know that God, in his infinite wisdom, has seen my greatness and will grant me the power to carry my birthright into the future.

I know this is true, for Mother has told me so. She has stopped visiting my room as she did when I was a child. Back then she would come, late at night, and sit at the edge of my bed, telling me all about my greatness.

"You come from a long line of wealth, Albert," she would croon, stroking my head. "You must always remember that you are special, and you must carry on this legacy. Everything you see was given to us as our due, for we are chosen to lead. And you, my son, shall lead the people."

I did not need Mother to tell me those things, but I was pleased that she recognized the truth. It was clear to me from my earlier days that I was special, as I was never burdened by the mortal encumbrance of emotions. I understand that others weep and cry, but I am not impeded by such bothers.

It is strange, as I am surrounded by those who are ignorant to who I am. I am given whatever I ask for, as is my due, and the servants never bother to look beyond the surface.

Except Josie.

I knew, instinctively, that I must hide my true self from this slave, for she had a fearsome sort of magic about her. I tried to tell Mother that Josie was a witch, but Mother simply laughed.

"If she is a witch, then use your own power and do away with her," Mother said.

Perhaps one day I will, but for now I will hide my true self and bide my time. Soon I will be old enough to enter the world of politics and use my influence upon the people. Despite our democracy, I shall be their ruler. The people are mindless enough that they will not recognize me as such.

Josie has told me that there is a child in my future, a child that will have a birthmark in the shape of a star on the back of his neck. She said this child will change my world and offer me a chance for a better future, a future that will save my soul. She said this child will have great power, and can help me or hurt me, that it would ultimately be my choice.

I do not believe Josie has the power to predict the future, but nonetheless, I shall watch for such a child. If one is born, I shall kill him, and the power shall remain with me.

And if this is the case, I shall have to kill Josie, too.

As mother said, I am destined to take my rightful place within society, and I cannot allow anything to get in the way.

Book 2

Margaret

*"Love is composed of a single soul
inhabiting two bodies."*
Aristotle

1795

Margaret

I may have been there, but all I know of my first real journey is what my mother told me. I have no memory of my four-year-old self crossing all that water, bound for a land that promised us a brighter future. How strange, I would learn later, that Josie and I came here on ships at 'round the same time. Slave ships but of a different hue.

"'Twas quite a smell," my mother would say. "Never before in all my life have I smelled anything that bad, and I was raised on a farm, mind you. All those people crammed in there, it wasn't natural." She would shake her head at this point in the story, and speak in a hushed tone. "All that death."

We sailed from County Cork, Ireland to Yorktown, Virginia, a voyage that, according to my mother, lasted longer than a full season. "It was winter when we left, and the sun was warm on my back by the time we got there," she told me. My mother, a skilled midwife and herbalist, had signed on to become an indentured servant in this new place, where she was promised money and goods at the end of her term. With a rapidly growing population, her services would prove useful in the new world.

When I asked her why we had to leave Ireland, she always said the same thing. "I didn't know what else to do," she admitted. "There weren't many choices for us."

As a young girl I was highly inquisitive, and often asked her questions about life, love, and God. Plus, I couldn't help but wonder what my life would have been like had we stayed behind.

"Were you in some sort of trouble?" I asked.

I remember her sad smile. "Only the sort of trouble that forces you into a life not of your own choosing, trouble that makes everything three times as hard as it should be and wears you down to the bone until there's nothing left. Even the banshees were comin' round at night, howling at us with their warnings from the dead. I wasn't going to stay and hear that for the rest of my life, which may not have been very long if the banshees had anything to say about it."

"What did the banshees tell you?"

"They told me of love mixed with sorrow, of a time that was comin' where the fires of hell would rage upon the lands of the earth, tearing souls apart and hurling them into the gray pit of purgatory."

Like any good Irish mother, mine could spin a tale.

"After your father died there weren't a whole lot of options for me," she said. "I could have stayed, but we had no more family, as everyone had gone north in search of work. We were starving, and I thought this would be my chance to give you a better life."

We were going to work for a Mr. Hamlee DePreux in Williamsburg, Virginia, a wealthy merchant who owned a tobacco farm. His house was much larger than what we had lived in previously, and there was an entirely separate building where all the cooking was done.

"Why don't they cook in the regular house?" I asked my mother.

"Fire," she said. "You don't want the house to catch fire. Burnin's a terrible way to die."

I was curious about everything, and followed my mother around all day as she worked. Gradually, I became her apprentice, learning about birthing and herbs, healing and medicines, living and dying.

It was a grand old house, with plenty of room for everyone, which was good since Mr. and Mrs. DePreux had seven children, as well as a large number of aunts, uncles and cousins living with them. There was always some sort of activity going on, which made it an exciting place to be.

My mother worked hard her entire life, choosing to stay with the DePreux family even after her servitude ended. "I like what I do," she told me. "And there are enough people in this house that need me, that's a fact." But despite all their hard work, people still gossiped about the indentured servants. From the time we got to America I remember hearing words like 'idle', 'lazy', and 'simple' whenever there was any mention of this segment of society.

When I was around ten years old, I overheard the kitchen women talking. "Keep an eye on her. Just because we haven't caught her stealing, doesn't mean she won't. Says her husband died back in the old country, but I think she just abandoned the poor man, stole the child and ran here."

My mother did not take kindly to that kind of talk about anyone, and she wasn't going to sit back and let someone say that about her. "Who do you think you're speaking of? Do you not have work to do yerself? Idle hands are fodder for the devil, as are wagging tongues that know not of what they say!" That stopped them from talking, and I never again heard anyone say anything bad about my mother. They had plenty to say about the other indentured servants, but my mother earned their respect that day.

I may have been the child of a servant but I felt as rich as anyone. There was never any doubt in my mind of my mother's love for me, and I never went hungry. My mother taught me as best she could, and I was reassured in knowing my path in life.

As a young woman of sixteen years, I was comforted with the knowledge that I, too, would become a midwife and herbalist. After all, I'd learned everything I needed to know about healing the sick. All I had to worry about was finding a suitable husband. Surely the day would come when I would find a love to spend my life with, or at least a suitable mate to give me children.

1817

Margaret

It is love, after all, that will damn me to the fires of hell.

I ran, ignoring the pain that lanced up my side, ignoring the fact that I could not catch my breath. I ran for my life, mine and my unborn child's. If he caught me, surely Albert would kill me, in the same way he'd killed his slave, Josie.

I could not think of Josie right now; kind, sweet Josie. I would not let the images slow me, images of Albert beating her, then taking her bound and gagged body and dumping her into the fire. Last night when I came to visit her she said she had a premonition that she was gonna see her mama. "She been a long time dead," she said. Then she told me the story about Africa, and visiting in the soul world in the underground place. Last thing she did was to give me her luck ball with the amulet she wore around her neck. "Keep this on you always," she said, tears streaming down her face. "I be watchin' you and that baby in your belly. You safe with this."

Josie had always feared the fire, ever since she had been disfigured saving Albert. And to die within that thing she feared the most, that type of ending to her life was the most ignoble of all.

Tears pricked at my eyes as the forest flashed around me, branches scratching at my face as I ran, heedless of whether or not there was a path before me. I dared not stop, but I was frantic about Albert, not knowing where he was. Was he behind me still? Had he somehow circled around, and was right now waiting for me up ahead?

I had to stop, if only to get my bearings and come up with a plan. I checked for the luck ball and the amulet. I didn't put a lot of faith in slave magic and medicine, but I believed in Josie. Standing with my back pressed against a tree, my skirts were tangled in my sweaty thighs as I tried to control my breathing. Listening, I could hear nothing. But I knew it would not be long before he found me, and when he did, my fate would be the same as Josie's.

I am a liability to this man I once loved. I have seen what he is capable of, and if I dare to speak of his actions it will ruin his political career. The fact that I am carrying Albert's child means nothing to him, and he will not hesitate to kill me. Maybe it is because I am with child that he wants to take my life.

I tilted my head upward, looking to the heavens for guidance. God, have mercy upon me, I do not want to die. I do not want my baby to die.

A gentle breeze caused the branches to sway, while sunlight broke through a cloud and filtered onto the mossy forest floor.

I smiled. *Thank you.*

Gathering my skirts, I tucked them up into my waistband, so that only my knickers showed. Not in the least bit ladylike, but I didn't have time for that sort of thing right now. Moving to a sturdy oak a few feet away, I grabbed hold of the bottom branch and began climbing. I climbed without looking down, up into the canopy of the tree that welcomed me into its leafy embrace.

The higher I climbed, the more the branches began to thin out. I had gone as far as I dared at about twenty feet, and stretched myself on my stomach along the length of a branch, with my feet resting at the trunk. If

I stayed balanced right there, I might survive the rest of this day.

It wasn't long before I heard him crashing through the undergrowth. "Margaret, darling, where are you?" he called. "Come out, dear, I just want to talk. I think you've misunderstood what you saw."

I held my breath, willing him not to look up. If he saw me, there was no escape.

"Margaret, let me know you're safe, let me know Josie didn't hurt you. I was so worried about you," he said.

I knew better. Josie would never hurt me, not in a million years. Josie had been Albert's slave, a nurse maid given to him as a child. His family had kept her on, vowing never to sell or trade her because she had saved his life.

And how did he repay his debt to this brave woman? I could not believe what I had witnessed moments earlier. Albert used the thing that terrified Josie most to control her.

Fire.

It was fire that Josie had saved him from, and it was fire that terrified her to no end. Albert knew that only too well. He tortured her first, threatening her by burning her with the flame from his torch. Then he set her ablaze, using the flames she feared above all else to exterminate her.

I still do not know if he did it out of anger at her prophecy or simply because he could. I do not understand the workings of his mind.

Unbidden, the tears streamed down my face, falling to the ground below.

The ground where Albert stood.

Horrified, I froze. Did my tears fall upon Albert? Would he think it was raining and look up? Surely, I was condemned.

He stood almost directly below me, surveying the land. His voice may have been full of sweetness and light, but I could see his face clearly. There was nothing sweet about the look on his face; in fact, it still held the murderous rage that I witnessed just a short time ago.

"You should not hide from me," he called. His voice was softer, but there was no mistaking the razor edge. "I will find you, Margaret, no matter what. I will search all the land over for you; I will not rest until I find you. Josie's prophecy will not hold true."

After another moment of standing below me, he walked away. I didn't let go of my breath for a full minute, wondering if he would return.

It would be a long night, but as long as I remained secure in the branches, I began to think I just might survive.

For now.

As comforting as I may find the sounds of the forest, sleeping on a tree branch is not the ideal place to bed. I didn't dare go to the ground, however, as I was still working out a plan in my mind.

That night I shed tears for Josie, myself, and my unborn child, the three people who were betrayed by Albert in the worst possible way.

In so many ways, Josie was a remarkable woman. A healer by nature, it was not surprising that she had sacrificed herself to save the young Albert. Josie had always been kind to me, a sort of mother figure that nurtured this young Irish immigrant full of hope for her future.

"Child, you gon' be jus' fine, wait and see. God's got somethin' special planned for you," she said to me all the time. I'd met Josie when I'd begun seeing Albert, the man I believed I loved.

"Don' go trustin' love, child," she warned. "You never know when you gonna need somethin' else."

I didn't always understand what this strange woman was telling me, but her intent was always clear. She was there to help and safeguard Albert and provide healing for others when she could. Slave medicine was frowned upon, but she said it was her gift from God and He would protect her.

I asked Albert about her once. "She seems so good, why do you ignore her?" I said.

"She's insane," he answered. "She claims to know the future. Crazy old woman. Now get over here, I have needs that must be met."

I remember the thrill of being in his arms, the shiver of anticipation I would get right before seeing him. I knew he came from a good family, and I wanted to please him so much.

"Why you wanna be somethin' you ain't?" Josie asked me one day.

"I want to be someone Albert will be proud of when he introduces me to his family," I answered.

Josie just shook her head. "You know there's no pleasin' that man, so don't get your hopes up about anything. If I was you, I wouldn't…" Sometimes Josie would start to say things, maybe try to warn me. But she never finished those things she started to say, and I knew better than to ask.

Even then, I realized there were things in this world I was better off not knowing.

The last time I saw Josie she was smiling at Albert, mocking him. "You can beat me all you want, Mr.

Albert," she said. "But there ain't nothin' gonna change the future. I've told your family before, and y'all never believed me, but it's the truth."

"That stupid prophecy that you've been spouting for years, you expect us to believe it? Shut your mouth," he roared. "Don't you dare speak ill of my family. You owe your life to us."

He was binding her body as he spoke, twisting the rope so tightly I wondered how she was still breathing.

"A child will be born," she began in a singsong voice. "A child born to you, and he shall be born of a woman who carries the magic of the old country within. This child will be the undoing of your family, Albert Hutchins, and you shall know him by the birthmark of the star on the back of his neck."

He struck her, hard, across the face. "You're nothing, you know that? I own you, and you're nothing."

My body began shaking as I witnessed the scene before me.

"And just so we're clear, it is you who owes your life to me." Those were Josie's last words to Albert before he dumped her into the roaring bonfire.

I drifted into an uneasy sleep, not fully slumbering, but dozing in the tree. Just before dawn, I dropped from my perch in the tree and made my way back to the forest floor, moving slowly so my stiffened legs would not give way.

I had had all night to think about my plan. There was only one thing to do. I must leave Williamsburg and find passage to my mother's brother who lived over the river in Gloucester. He was my Uncle Mike, a man I had never met, but whom I must now beg for mercy.

It was no longer just my life at stake.

1819

Margaret

How could I not laugh as I watched Quincy and the puppy chase each other round in circles? Despite the solemnity of the day, a small child and a dog could not fail to bring a smile to my face.

I alternated between watching my young son from the window of the house and watching my Uncle Mike lying on a bed we had set up in the sitting room. The bed had only been in place for a couple weeks, and I knew it would not be there much longer.

"Margaret, love, we need to talk." Uncle Mike's voice was raspy and weak, but his tone was determined. I kept my eyes fixed upon the outside scene until I knew I would spill no tears.

"More water?" I asked, keeping my voice bright.

"No. Come, sit with me for a moment," he said. "There are things I have to say, and I must tell you now, before my time is up."

"Don't say that," I cried. "You'll get better… you have to…" I knew the truth, but did not accept it. Honestly, I could barely stand the thought of a life without Uncle Mike. He'd provided me with not just shelter, but a real home, a refuge full of love and warmth for me and Quincy at a time when we needed it most. I didn't know how we would survive alone.

"Sit next to me, child," he said. I obeyed, knowing he was right. His time here on Earth was drawing to a close, and we had to talk. Before he could speak, however, he was seized by a fit of coughing.

"Let me make you more tea," I said. "Perhaps I can ease some of your pain."

He nodded, speaking once the coughing stopped. "Your remedies are a boon, and surely have saved me from the pain that is constant. I don't know what I'd have done without you."

I shook my head, mostly to prevent the tears again. The futility of it was disheartening, but I knew weeks ago that I could not save Uncle Mike. My extensive knowledge of herbal remedies could only cure certain things; this was the one thing that had no cure. I'd felt the lumps beneath his skin myself, and I knew they had multiplied. I also knew it was killing him.

I made my way outside, stopping in the yard to hug Quincy before going to the tiny outbuilding that housed the kitchen. The sun was shining and it was a beautiful day, an irony if ever there was one. While in the kitchen I added kindling to the fire and prepared another tea with the Valerian root I'd been able to procure. It came from overseas, so I'd had to beg and bargain with the local grocer to obtain as much as I had. It was the only thing that kept Uncle Mike's pain at bay.

When I returned to the sitting room Uncle Mike's eyes were closed. I placed the cup at his bedside, not wanting to disturb him, and sat in the chair next to his bed where I could continue to watch him while looking out the window.

"Nobody ever knew, my dear," he said, eyes still closed.

I smiled. "That's because they all believe you'd never lie."

"I've only done what I had to do to protect my family. God rest your mother's soul, it's what she herself would have done."

When I'd arrived in Gloucester that dark, rainy day, I showed up at Uncle Mike's house with only the clothes on my back. He took me in without question. In the first few days of my stay with him, I did not venture outside. I don't believe anyone knew of my arrival, but it wouldn't be long before word spread of the niece that had shown up in the small hamlet. Over the course of two days I told him my story, although it shamed me to do so. I knew I didn't have much time before my pregnancy began to show.

For the rest of my days, I shall not forget his response. Cradling my face in his hands, he told me, "From this point forward you are my widowed niece, your husband having been killed because of the incompetency of that idiot, Brigadier General William Hull. You shall live with me in respectability, and you will be safe here."

That is exactly what happened. The townspeople of Gloucester did not question my Uncle's story, and accepted me and my son as part of the society there. They never knew that I had managed to escape from the evil that tried to hold me in Williamsburg, using what little money I had saved to buy a boat ride across the river.

I flourished in Gloucester, feeling like I was part of the community. I had learned well from my mother, and my proficiency as a midwife and herbalist became well known. I was often called upon to help deliver babies or soothe a fever.

Now, when I needed it most, my skills had failed me.

"There's nothing to be done, dear," Uncle Mike said. "I'm going to die, and that's fine."

"Forgive me, Uncle, but I do not agree. I don't think it's fine at all."

Uncle Mike smiled, eyes still closed. "The one thing to remember is that there is always healing to be had, no matter what the disease. The difficult thing to accept is that sometimes the only way to be healed is through death."

I knew he was right, of course. I just didn't want to let him go. "I'll miss you," I whispered.

"Be excited for me, dear, as I am about to embark upon the grandest adventure of all, into the great beyond. What do you think lies ahead for my spirit?"

I wasn't certain if he was serious or not. "The bible says –"

"Never mind that," he interrupted. "Nothing more than a bunch of stories put out there to scare us, keep us all in line."

I tried to hide a smile. "You know you're putting your soul in jeopardy, saying things like that."

"But it made you smile, so it was worth it." His words were followed by paroxysms of coughing. I stood to give him his tea, but he waved at me to sit down. When he was finally able to talk, he held onto my hand with a firm grip. "Child, I might be old and frail, but my mind is still sharp. I knew this time was fast approaching, and I've made arrangements."

I started to shake my head, then stopped. He was right; these were things I needed to know. Whether or not I wanted to know was another story, but we didn't have the luxury of me falling apart right now.

"Go on," I said.

"My last will and testament is in the old wooden box on top of my dresser," he said. "And, just in case, there's another rolled up and stored in the cupboard, behind the fine china."

"Behind the fine china?"

He smiled. "Exactly. Who would think to look there? Anyway, you have to keep the copy safe after you file the original with the courthouse. I don't want that impertinent scoundrel to try and pull any of his shenanigans."

My anxiety rose a notch. "What have you done?"

"Only what needed to be done. I cannot see the future, love, so I have no way of knowing what's going to happen, but as of right now the only way a man can have any life at all is if he's a landowner."

Another coughing fit seized him, and I waited until it subsided. Like it or not, there was nothing more I could do for Uncle Mike.

"I've left this property to Quincy. I didn't dare leave it to you, love, as I knew it would be overturned by the courts if Albert ever got wind of this. At least now your son will be a landowner, and will have all the rights that come with that."

A landowner. It was more than I'd ever dared to dream of for my son's future. I looked out the window, watching as my son lay curled on the grass next to his dog. The two of them must have been exhausted.

A quick gasp came from Uncle Mike, and when I turned back to his bed he gripped my hand even tighter. Closing his eyes, I listened to his labored breathing, knowing we were near the end.

Uncle Mike would die today.

1828

Nathaniel

When I'm preparing for a speech, I walk with my head down, rehearsing my words in my head. It is this habit that changed my life.

I knew I had to impart my message that day with sincerity and vigor. The people needed to understand what was at stake, and it was vital that I convey to them the importance of the right to vote for all men, not just those who owned land. In my position as an elected official I understood the worth of allowing the masses to vote.

I swear, I never saw her coming.

One moment I was looking at the ground, the next there were bottles and trinkets flying everywhere, landing next to the most beautiful creature that ever existed. The background noises that I had been dimly aware of, the horse carts, water lapping at the shore and crowd conversations were replaced by a rushing noise that filled my head.

Her steel-gray eyes were full of anger, and her luscious mouth was compressed into a thin line. Without a word, she stood, brushed her skirt, and began gathering her things.

"Excuse me, Miss, I did not see you," I said, dropping to my knees to help gather her belongings.

"Obviously," she answered, taking a dark green bottle filled with liquid out of my hands. "Thank you, I can gather my own effects."

"But it's my fault, let me help you," I said. A small part of my mind registered that she wasn't classically pretty, but the combination of big, round eyes, freckled face and gleaming dark hair was perfect. She was, perhaps, too thin, and I couldn't help but wonder if she had enough food on her dinner table.

A husband that could not provide for her, perhaps?

A quick glance at her left hand showed no rings, and I let out a breath. "Can I help you with anything?" I asked.

"No, just let me pass," she said, standing straight and fixing me with a direct stare.

"Do I know you?" I know it was a silly thing to ask, but for one fleeting moment I had the sense that I'd seen this woman before. I don't know where I could have known her from, as we were obviously from different stations in life. Not that any of that mattered to me. As long as I could continue to gaze into the depths of her eyes, I knew I would be happy forever.

"No," she said, attempting to walk away.

Before I could say a word, a whirlwind came rushing behind me, yelling.

"Mother! Are you alright? I saw you fall."

A smile softened her face, making her appear radiant. "I'm fine, Quincy," she said. "This man and I simply bumped into each other by accident."

A boy of perhaps ten years old looked up into my face. Watching him, I saw the same upturned nose with a splatter of freckles. I couldn't help but smile. "Hello, young sir," I said, extending my hand. "I am so terribly sorry to have caused your mother distress. As sometimes happens when I'm thinking of other things, I was not watching where I was going. Please accept my apologies."

The boy nodded, solemn. "That happens to me, too. Momma says I have my head in the clouds sometimes."

"That's enough, Quincy," she said. Her voice was gentle yet firm. "We have to be going now."

I couldn't let this exquisite creature leave yet. "My name is Nathaniel Parker," I told them. "I'm running for office here – "

"I know who you are, Mr. Parker," she interrupted. "We really must be going now. Come along, son."

She began to walk away from me, so I walked alongside her. "I'm giving a speech down by the docks in a little while, if you'd like to come and listen."

"I don't see that having me listen to you would do you any good, Mr. Parker," she said. "It's not like I can vote for you."

"No, but you'd get a better idea of who I am and what I stand for," I said. I knew that if my dear mother were standing beside me she surely would have dragged me away to keep me from speaking to this woman. Mother had her own ideas of what I should be doing with my life, but I tended to ignore her whenever possible.

She stopped and turned to me. "You are a politician, are you not?"

For some reason she was angry, and I wasn't sure what I had done wrong. "Yes, ma'am, I am a politician. My platform –"

"I don't need to know anything about your platform," she interrupted. "If you are a politician, I know everything I need to know."

And with that, she walked away.

Margaret

A politician. Of course, that would explain why the man was so utterly rude. From the moment he collided with me to his most impertinent questions, it was everything I could do to hold myself in place while trying to escape.

I knew what his type was like, with his good looks and his charm. I had a son to protect, and I would not fall into that trap again.

As I hurried away, I heard a voice calling my name. "Miss Margaret, wait please." Turning, I saw Mac McCormick, the local deputy. He tipped his hat as he walked over to where I stood.

Mac was a tall, broad shouldered man, slightly older than me. I'd known him since I first moved to

Gloucester, and what I had first mistaken for shyness was actually a kind of quiet strength. Uncle Mike had always said I could trust Mac, and I believed it. He stood on the right side of the law, and I knew he would always be fair. Still, I never trusted him enough to tell him about Albert.

Besides Uncle Mike, I never trusted anyone enough to tell them about Albert.

"Forgive me, Margaret, I don't mean to intrude. I couldn't help notice Nathaniel talking to you. Was he bothering you?" Mac asked.

Sounds like he knows Mr. Parker. Interesting.

Looking up into his blue eyes, I answered. "No, I'm fine. It was simply a small mishap, thank you."

"You let me know if he gives you any trouble. I won't have it," Mac said.

Before I could think of the implications of the question, I asked, "Are you acquainted with him?"

"He certainly is," the voice behind me answered. Despite the fact that we had only exchanged a minimum of words, I already knew that voice.

"Did you follow me?" I demanded.

Nathaniel smiled at me, and I couldn't help thinking that he looked a little sad.

"No, ma'am, I did not follow you. As I mentioned earlier, I am on my way to the dock to give a speech."

Looking from me to Mac, Nathaniel nodded. "Mac, how are you?"

"Fine."

A tense silence stood in the air, broken by Quincy leaning in to whisper to me. "Momma, can I go play with my friends?" I looked in the direction he was pointing to see a gaggle of children playing with a ball.

Nodding, I told him, "Yes, but make sure you don't wander off without letting me know where you're going." Turning back to the men, I inclined my head. "Gentlemen, good day." My intention was to leave, as it was obvious there was some sort of ill will between the two men. As I started to walk away, Nathaniel tried to stop me.

"Wait –"

Before he could even take a step in my direction, however, Mac brought his arm back and punched Nathaniel. I heard a popping sound as Mac's fist connected with Nathaniel's nose.

In the moment after it happened, everything around us stopped. Even the birds were silent. As expected, blood gushed everywhere, soaking Nathaniel's shirt.

I didn't like him, but I couldn't let him remain in pain. "Here," I said, stepping forward with a rag I had produced from my satchel. "Use this to apply pressure. I have some capsicum in here; give me a moment to find it."

"You have what?" they asked simultaneously.

I didn't even look up from my bag. "Something to help the bleeding. Here it is," I said, producing a small brown bottle. "You'll need to take this with water."

Nathaniel shook his head. "Dus' gib it to be," he said, unable to speak clearly with his nose blocked.

I had to warn him. "You should not take –"

"Gib it to be!" he insisted.

I looked at Mac, who shrugged. "Go ahead and give it to him, he needs a little help."

I had no earthly idea what had provoked Mac to hit this man, but I knew Mac to be fair and honest. If he felt it necessary to hit someone, then this person was probably not a good person to begin with, I reasoned. So, giving him a dose of capsicum, also known as cayenne pepper, without water, might be allowable.

Silently I measured a dose and handed it to Nathaniel, who swallowed it without hesitation. I watched, waiting for his reaction. To his credit, he swallowed several times and I saw his eyes water, but he said nothing. Of course, it was possible he could not speak at that moment.

"What did you give him?" Mac asked.

"Cayenne pepper," I said. "It's useful for stopping nosebleeds." I could see Mac try to hold his laughter back, covering his mouth with his hand. His face grew almost as red as Nathaniel's.

Finally, Mac said, "Without any water?"

Trying to fix a look of pure innocence on my face, I told him, "You both insisted."

A gasping noise escaped from Nathaniel. "I'm fine," he said. "Just fine. I simply need to clean up before I have to give my speech." He nodded at Mac. "I deserved that. You have to know how sorry I am. If you'd like, you can do it again."

I could only stare at this man who still had a trickle of blood coming from his nose and a bruise under his left eye that was starting to swell. He was being terribly gracious about the whole thing.

Mac shook his head. "I've wanted to do that for a long time, but it doesn't make anything better. I certainly feel the same, no better, no worse."

"If I had seen you, I would have offered my face to you for a beating. Every time I pass you on the street you turn and walk away," Nathaniel said.

"Would either of you care to tell me what this is about?" I asked. "Plus, Nathaniel, you owe me five pence."

Nathaniel smiled. "Yes, ma'am. I'll have it sent directly to your home, if you tell me where you live."

"Margaret, don't trust him," Mac warned.

"Margaret? That's a beautiful name," Nathaniel said. "But before we go any further, let me tell you a story." He paused for a moment, looking to the distance and drawing in a breath. "Years ago, Mac and I were the best of friends."

Mac muttered something, looking at the ground.

"Mac?" I said. "I don't need to hear this."

"But I need to tell it," Nathaniel answered. I understood what he meant, and I knew intuitively that this was a moment of healing for all. I remained silent, bearing witness to what he had to say. "Mac and my sister, Catherine, were in love. Deeply in love. The kind of love that comes along once in a lifetime, the kind of love that should be treasured, nurtured, and protected."

In the entire time I'd known Mac, he was an unmarried man. "What happened to Catherine?" I asked.

Nathaniel shook his head. "It happened before she got sick. I believe she got sick because – well, let me tell this in order. My mother is a bit… domineering. She has expectations of her family, and has instilled in us that we must live up to the family name."

I could not stop the shudder from coursing through my body. What this man was telling me was so similar to Albert's family that I began to fear, in earnest, for my safety.

Surely, Mac would not let anything untoward happen?

I don't think Nathaniel noticed my discomfort. He continued to tell his story, looking directly at Mac as he spoke. "You must understand, this happened almost ten years ago. I was young enough, naïve enough, to believe that I could change things. I believed that if I were to be honest with my family and told them the truth, then I could save my sister."

"Save her from the likes of me, right?" Mac growled.

Nathaniel shook his head. "No. I know that's what you've thought all these years, but it's not what I had in mind. I thought I could stop you both from leaving, keep you here with our family. I believed that once I told my parents about your love, they would welcome you into our home."

Mac frowned. "You know your mother would never have approved of the likes of me. I was not good enough, I had no money, and my family name meant nothing. What were you thinking?"

"I was thinking that if they understood about your love, they would overlook all that," Nathaniel said. "It was foolish, I can see that now. But in my youth, I believed love would conquer all."

There was a deep silence as the two men regarded each other across a short space of dirt. Finally, I had to know. "What happened to Catherine?" I asked.

"Consumption," Mac spit the word out. "They told me she died of consumption."

"She died with your name on her lips," Nathaniel whispered. "And I am sorry for any role I played in keeping you apart. I thought –"

"You thought wrong," Mac yelled. His face turned completely red, and for a moment I thought he may have been suffering from heart failure. "You thought that with your privilege and money you could turn it all around and make things work out? Your arrogance is unbelievable, both you and your family. I hope you burn in hell."

Nathaniel's face had gone white as he watched Mac storm off. Turning to me, he began to offer an apology. "Please, accept my apology for what you just heard. That's no type of language to use in front of a lady."

Clearly, Nathaniel was suffering from his ill-fated attempts to help his sister and her lover, and for some reason I believed that he truly had their best interests at heart. It was a touching story, and one that at any other time I might have asked more questions about. But I had run out of time. The blood in my veins turned to ice as I looked across the crowded street to where my child was playing with the other children.

Albert was standing directly behind Quincy, watching his every move.

Quincy

I could barely believe my eyes when I saw what Elijah had in his hand. I didn't know anyone else who had one, much less the three that Elijah was holding out for us to look at. I was in awe, as were my friends Adam and Henry.

Cupped in Elijah's hand were three glass marbles. They were magnificent.

"Can we play with them?" Adam asked.

"Can we use them with our marbles?" Henry said. Of the two, Henry sounded doubtful. "They probably work lots better than my clay marbles, so it wouldn't be fair."

"Who cares?" I said. "It'll be fun to compare them with each other."

So we drew our circle in the dirt, and set about comparing the clay marbles to the glass ones. We were methodical in our quest to determine which was better, and so absorbed in what we were doing that I hardly noticed when Hope came over and crouched down beside us.

"Quincy," she whispered.

"What?" I said. I was so caught up with the marbles I didn't even look up from my game.

"You're mother is gonna whoop you," Henry said.

"Henry Alstead, will you hush for one moment," Hope said. "Quincy, I have something to tell you."

"Why don't you talk normal?" Elijah asked.

"Wait till your mother sees how you got your dress all messy from kneeling in the dirt," Henry said. "I remember the last time you came over and played with us, she showed up and dragged you off by your ear. You're gonna get it for sure. You should probably do something about that."

Henry was right. Hope's mother was a little touched in the head, I think, and she was always going on and on about something or other that none of us could understand. We liked Hope, and hated to see some of the beatings she took from her mother.

"I'll leave in a minute," she said. "But first, listen to me. Quincy, there's a man been following you. He's standing there, watching you. I think he's downright evil, maybe came from the crossroads or something."

For a moment, I thought maybe Hope had caught the same thing her mother had. What in tarnation was that girl talking about? It didn't make any sense. But when I looked up at her, she nodded her head a little, indicating something behind and to her right. Sure enough, when I looked behind her, there was someone standing there, staring at me.

She was right. His eyes were dark, black pits that burned into me. There was no question that it was me he was looking at, too. My heart started beating wildly, but I was trapped, pinned by his gaze.

As if from a distance, I could hear Henry's voice. "Crim – in – ny…"

The next thing I knew, a strong hand clamped down upon my shoulder, pulling me up off the ground.

Nathaniel

I had to act quickly. Margaret's fear was palpable, and when I saw the source of it I knew she had good reason. Albert Hutchins was not a man whose threats could be taken lightly; I knew enough about Albert to know he was a danger to any who crossed him.

Apparently, Margaret had crossed him.

"Wait here," I told her. "I'll get the boy. Don't let Albert see you."

"What do you know of this?" she asked.

"I know Albert, and that's all I need to know."

She looked like she was about to argue with me, so I leaned close to speak to her. "Listen to me," I said. "It's clear that you are afraid of him, and it's clear that he has his eye on your child. Let me help you. I know Albert, and I know what he is capable of."

She searched my face, looking, I'm sure, for a sign of trustworthiness. I knew she had to take me on faith, so I clasped her hands in mine and gave them a squeeze. After a moment, she nodded.

"I'll make my speech, and then take the boy to my home. You can meet us there. If you leave now, it won't take you long to get there. Do you know where Rosewood Hall is?"

"Yes, the large house on the river," she said.

"Good. Try to stay off the main road, though. Albert won't hurt the boy if he is with me, but if he finds you walking alone…" I didn't have to finish my sentence. I think both of us knew that no good would come of Albert finding her walking, alone, to my house.

I hurried over to where her boy, Quincy, was playing, and grabbed him by the shoulder. "Let's go," I said. "It's time to get to work."

To my surprise, he didn't struggle, and didn't ask questions. A young girl was standing near the circle where they had been playing, and she nodded solemnly. "Good thing you came, Mr. Parker," she said. I smiled at her, trying for all the world to pretend everything was normal. I didn't know the specifics of why Albert wanted the boy, but it was clear from the look on his face that he was enraged.

Quincy and I had only taken two steps away from the area when Albert's voice rang out. "Wait one moment, please, Mr. Parker." It was a voice filled with malicious intent, a voice I would know anywhere.

"Good day, Mr. Hutchins," I said, keeping my hand clamped firmly on Quincy's shoulder. "If you will excuse us, please, we must be on our way. We have work to see to."

"All in good time," Albert said. "First, I would like to have a word with the boy."

"No," I said. I knew Albert was an officious little man, and I knew he was cruel. But at that point his condescending tone provoked my anger. Who was he to speak to me in such a manner?

"Mr. Hutchins, I know not what your business is with this boy, or why you desire to see him, but he is with me for right now. You will simply have to wait."

Before I realized what was happening, Albert's hand whipped out and spun the boy around. Grabbing the hair on the back of his head, he lifted the hair off the boy's neck. I could see his neck had a star-shaped birthmark, a stain upon his fair skin.

Albert paled, taking a step backward. I used that opportunity to pull the boy back to me, throwing an arm across his small chest to protect him. "If you will excuse us, now, Mr. Hutchins," I said, not fully expecting him to fall back.

Albert smiled then, a smile of malice and ill intent. "Of course," he said, bowing. "I know who you are, young man, and I must say I am so glad to have finally met you." Albert began to walk away, turned back, and spoke to us.

"Tell your mother I said hello, and that I'll be seeing her again. Soon."

Margaret

The short amount of time between leaving my son behind with Nathaniel and when they caught up to me was the longest ninety minutes of my life. I knew Albert meant to harm us, and I had to trust this stranger.

I berated myself the entire time I trudged toward his house. How did I know I could trust Nathaniel? All I had were my instincts, and I felt certain that he was an honorable man. But, as I well knew, my instincts had failed me before, so it was possible I was wrong and had put my son's life in danger.

It was too late to change anything now. I had to keep moving, and have faith. I knew what Albert was capable of, and apparently so did others. Uncle Mike was wise to create a copy of his final wishes. In 1820 the Gloucester courthouse burned, and all the records burned with it. People around here remarked what a tragedy the fire had been, but I knew the truth of it. I knew it was born from one man's desire to destroy a future that had been predestined.

As Nathaniel had suggested, I kept off the road, but I could still see travelers from my path. I heard the sound of the horses before I saw them, and I crouched down low near a brush pile so I would not be seen.

I recognized the man driving the carriage immediately, and ran to the road to greet them. "Quincy!"

Nathaniel pulled on the reins to halt the horses, and climbed down. "Let me help you in," he said. "I drove as slowly as I dared, hoping to find you."

With his assistance, I climbed into the carriage and grabbed hold of my son, hugging him and struggling to hold back my tears. For once, my young son was quiet, asking no questions and allowing me to hold him as I'd done when he was a baby.

The ride to Rosewood Hall took less time than I expected, perhaps because Nathaniel drove the carriage as fast as he dared. Bringing us around to the back of the house, he ushered us into the kitchen, set away from the main building. Near the blazing fire, an old black woman stood over a pot, stirring something that smelled like old river water. She looked up at us, and I saw that her eyes were filmy, but her wrinkled face was kind. I saw Quincy wrinkle his nose, and I spoke quietly into his ear. "Don't say a word, son. These people are trying to help us, and we don't want to insult them."

"Maude, what on earth is that smell?" Nathaniel asked. I saw Quincy try to suppress a smile.

"Tis something your mother asked me to do. I don't care for it, and I won't be doing it again," Maude answered.

"Thank the good Lord for small favors," Nathaniel muttered, perhaps not realizing that we had heard him. It was then that I, too, had to suppress a smile, and Nathaniel saw me cover my mouth with my hand.

"It is most definitely not a smell many would like to live with, is it?" he asked, smiling back at me.

"Certainly not," I answered.

"Although, perhaps I could have used some of that liquid when I took your remedy earlier," he teased.

I blushed then, remembering his nose and how it had bled. "Your nose is fine now, is it not?" I asked.

"But what happened to your shirt?" Maude asked. "And why are you in my kitchen?"

Nathaniel turned back to her. "How can you see my shirt, Maude? Sometimes I think you employ magic when you need it."

"Never you mind what I know and don't know," she answered. "Tell me what you came to say."

Clearly Nathaniel trusted this woman, as was evidenced by his next words. "I need you to keep these two busy, either in the kitchen or in the main house, but they need to be out of sight."

"Are they in some kind of trouble?" Maude said.

"No," he said. "But they are getting ready to ride with me on the campaign trail."

I tried to hide my surprise, as I didn't want my son to see my apprehension. Campaign trail? What was he planning?

Nathaniel saw the look in my eyes, and put his hands on my shoulders. "I'm going to help you get away from him. I don't know what he wants with you, but I do know that man is evil."

I made a decision to trust him. I didn't like it, but I knew I was out of options. Albert was hunting us, and I had to do whatever I could to keep Quincy safe. "Where are we going?" I asked.

"Richmond," he said. "We leave in the morning."

Nathaniel

It made my heart glad to see Margaret smile when I mentioned the pepper, in spite of her circumstances. But as much as I wanted to keep that smile on her face, we had to talk.

"Maude, why don't you take Quincy out to the garden to gather vegetables?"

Maude shot me a knowing look, then nodded. Turning from the pot of foul smelling liquid, she spoke to Margaret. "You're the medicine woman, ain't ya?"

Margaret smiled. "Yes. I learned most of what I know from my dear Irish mother, but I've been practicing here in Gloucester for almost a decade."

"Heard good things about you. You helped my friend, Nell, when she had that bout o' the flu."

"I remember her," Margaret said. "How is she? It's been a while since I've seen her."

"Fit as a fiddle," Maude said. Walking past me, she began to shepherd Quincy out the door. "Come along with old Maude, child, we'll go see if any of the squash is ready for harvest yet." She stopped, and turned to me. "Take care of that one. She's special." Without another word, she and the boy left the kitchen.

I took a breath and turned to Margaret. "So, perhaps we should talk," I said. I could see she made an effort not to wring her hands, an admirable show of self-restraint.

She must be terrified.

"Dare I ask why Albert is coming after you?" I said.

I could see her internal struggle as a range of emotions played over her face. Finally, she answered. "I think it might be best if you did not know. This will prevent you from inadvertently being put in danger."

"Albert is devious, I'll grant you that much. But as far as me being in danger from him, have no fear of that. Our families are known to each other, and have been for years." I paused, wondering how I was going to say what I had to say. "My mother and Albert's mother are the best of friends, so I'm certain no harm will come to me."

Margaret gave a snort. On most women it would be very unladylike, but on her it was a sign of utter disregard for social status. My heart beat wildly, and I yearned to reach out and touch a lock of her hair. "After the story you told me about Mac and your sister, it sounds like being friends with your mother is akin to being friends with Edward Teach," she said.

"You mean Blackbeard, the pirate?"

"Yes. Blackbeard was known for being shrewd and calculating, and your mother... well, she sounds similar. I'll bet your father just goes along with whatever she wants, doesn't he?"

It hadn't taken Margaret long to figure out my family dynamics. Perhaps that was for the best. I didn't plan on having a wasted life, like Mac and Catherine. When I should be lucky enough to fall in love, I planned on building a lifetime of happiness, and never letting go. Looking into Margaret's eyes, I realized I could finally begin planning for the rest of my life. First, I had to convince her to have me.

"If you ever want to talk about Albert, I'm here to listen. Do you have any relatives in Gloucester?"

She shook her head. "No, there was only my Uncle Mike, and he passed on some eight years ago."

"Was he a landowner?" I asked.

"Yes," she answered slowly, no doubt wondering why I asked.

"And do you still live in his house?" I wanted to know everything I could about this lovely woman, so I decided to start with the basics. Perhaps she would tell me more at some point, but I would wait and see on that.

We talked for a bit, and she told me her story in bits and pieces. I knew there were parts she was leaving out, but that was fine. The important thing was that she was comfortable with me.

"I am determined to see more people gain the right to vote," I told her as we sat at the long table in the kitchen. "I see my political role as one of creating opportunities for all peoples, not just landowning peoples. That's why I am going to Richmond, to deliver a speech at the capitol. I am scheduled to talk in one week's time. It's a perfect opportunity for you to get away from Albert and have some time to think about your future."

She looked uncertain. "I don't want to appear ungrateful, but I'm not sure it would be acceptable for us to travel alone with you. It might appear that we are –" She stammered and blushed, and I thought I'd never seen a lovelier sight.

"I would never ask anything improper of you," I said. "You will travel in one of the carriages behind me, with the others who are escorting me as part of my entourage."

She blinked, apparently surprised by the notion. "Your entourage?"

I nodded. "Yes, all the people who work with me to help keep things running smoothly. I can't do it all myself, you know. The trip will take several days, and we'll stop along the way to rest in the evenings." I could see the flicker of apprehension that still lingered. "I'll see to it that both you and Quincy are well taken care of," I said.

Lifting her eyes to mine, she finally smiled. "I suppose that settles it, then. We're off to Richmond."

Margaret

Our trip to Richmond was perhaps the most fun I'd ever had in my entire life. Quincy and I were treated like members of the family, and I was able to assist several times when members of our party came down with various ailments.

I could see Nathaniel winning Quincy over, and I watched as my son began to look to Nathaniel as a father figure.

It was so very unlike me to turn my trust over to someone I did not know, but it was Josie who convinced me to do so. Yes, long-dead Josie had been speaking to me at night, in my dreams.

She came to me as a healthy, vibrant woman, exuding warmth and love. "Margaret, do not fear Nathaniel, for he means you no harm. He will guide you and help you through this. Trust that even when things seem to be at their worst, there is a plan. Everything is unfolding in accordance with the Universal laws, and love will guide the way."

I wasn't certain I understood entirely, but I trusted Josie. And I knew that whenever she appeared in my dreams it was because she needed to speak with me. There was no doubt in my mind that she was, indeed, speaking with me.

This comforted me greatly, because the one dark spot upon our trip was my forgetful moment. I don't know how I had managed to do this, but somehow I had left behind my luck ball and amulet that Josie had given me.

To believe that those were the things that would keep me safe was a silly notion, yet there was a piece of me that grew distinctly uncomfortable with the thought of not wearing these pieces. Josie had warned me when she gave them to me, and I'd been careless and left them at my home in Gloucester.

But I must not think of that now. Just for now, I would focus on my son. And Nathaniel.

I enjoyed getting to know Nathaniel. He was a smart, funny, and kind person. He did everything he could to make Quincy and me comfortable, and for that I was grateful. The other members of our party accepted both of us without question, following Nathaniel's lead and treating us like family.

It was, perhaps, the happiest time of my life, a time when I felt momentarily safe and yes, loved.

If there is one lesson I have learned in this lifetime, it is that nothing good can last. When we arrived in Richmond, Nathaniel's schedule was hectic. Until that moment, I did not realize that a politician must always be working, no matter where he is. There were speeches and dinners, picnics and handshaking, and long talks between men. And through it all, Nathaniel insisted I stand by his side, his way of announcing his intentions to the world. Late at night, when darkness hid most people from themselves, Nathaniel would find me, whispering to me of his love and devotion, promising me all the things that I so wanted, things I yearned for in my life.

He never laid a hand on me, and I believed every word he said. It had only been days, but I knew he was a good man, a man who would guide us and keep us safe. I knew I could be with Nathaniel, and Quincy and I would settle into a life of benign happiness.

I dared, for the first time in years, to re-imagine my future.

And then my worst fear was realized.

The late September morning air was still and heavy as Nathaniel and I wandered through City Park hand in hand. The light of the rising sun reflected off the pond, creating an idyllic setting. When I turned to speak to Nathaniel I saw him.

It's true… blood makes noise. There was a ringing in my ears as the blood pounded through my veins, fear soaking my soul.

There, standing before us, was Albert. He was clutching Quincy, and I knew without being told that he would kill my son with little thought for taking a life.

Even his own son's life.

I opened my mouth to scream, but no sound came out. Nathaniel grabbed hold of my hand, and took a step in front of me to create a shield. I wanted to drop to my knees and cry, but I knew not to show any weakness. I had to be strong. I would not let Albert win.

"Come with me," Albert said. Without waiting for a reply, he turned and began walking. I had no choice, he had my son, and he let us see the knife he held at Quincy's back.

We followed him through the streets of Richmond, and the further we walked the more disoriented I became. Soon, I could smell the river air, and I assumed we were down by the docks of the James River. Within minutes I knew my assumptions were correct, as I could see the water in front of us.

"We're going for a ride," Albert said, inclining his head toward the steamboat that sat waiting at the dock.

"On the Merryville?" Nathaniel asked. "Whatever for? Why should we go there?"

Albert smiled at us, a cold, cruel smile that I remembered from the last time I saw Josie, just before he burned her to death. "I like the boat," he said. "And since I've reserved a room on board, I thought it would afford us some privacy to speak freely. After all, there are some things that need to be cleared up, aren't there, my dear?"

I would not let him see my fear. "I have nothing to say to you," I told him.

Without taking his eyes off me, Albert addressed Nathaniel. "Have you not wondered who fathered this child?"

Quincy, bless his soul, struggled to be free of Albert. "My father died fighting in the War of 1812," he said. "Let me go."

Albert laughed. "He did, did he? That's a very touching story, child."

The entire time we were walking toward the boat I could see Nathaniel trying to find a way to overtake Albert, but he dare not risk Quincy's life. Down the boat ramp we walked, while the crew stood alongside the Merryville Commerce, waiting for us to board.

"Everyone on board, mate?" Albert asked the first mate.

Yes, sir, we were only waiting for you and your guests to come aboard."

"Fine. Give us a minute to get to our rooms," Albert said.

He moved quickly, as if he knew the ship well, and we followed him as he disappeared down the steps that led below the deck. Moving into a hallway, Albert opened a door and vanished. I rushed to the doorway in time to see him turn and plunge the knife into Quincy's stomach.

"No!" I screamed.

Nathaniel came charging through and grabbed Albert by his shirt, dragging him away from Quincy. I kneeled down at Quincy's side, trying to staunch the flow of blood.

"It's okay, Momma. I'll be fine," my boy said.

"Yes, yes you will," I answered, not letting myself believe anything different.

I looked up to see Nathaniel and Albert fighting, and Albert broke free and came toward me, waving his bloody knife. Nathaniel was not fast enough, and Albert cut me in the upper arm, slashing me deeply several times.

"Momma!"

"Shhh, it's going to be alright," I whispered. It wasn't, and at that moment I knew in my heart we would die on that ship, but I wanted to remain peaceful for Quincy. It was all I could do for him now.

The men were fighting like dogs, throwing punches and snarling at each other. Nathaniel managed to drag Albert out the door, and I knew it was his intention to keep Albert away from us. I sat and held Quincy, wondering how long we had.

Suddenly, the ship gave a lurch. "Momma?"

"I think we're moving," I said, not knowing what was happening. Quincy and I were losing blood rapidly, and the floor around us was awash in red.

"I love you, baby," I said.

"Love you too, Momma."

That was when the white light exploded all around us.

Richmond Times-Dispatch
October 1, 1828

The Merryville Commerce

It is with great distress that we write of the following incident upon which occurred late night September 30, 1828, on the river known by all as the James River in the Commonwealth of Virginia. As the great steamship The Merryville Commerce began her voyage that day along the river there came about an explosion within the middle engines, causing a good portion of the boat to become engulfed in flames. Of the eighty passengers, none survived the horrendous explosion. More than twenty bodies were immediately thrown to their watery graves.

A surviving crew member reports seeing passengers struggle with each other on deck directly prior to the event. "I don't rightly know what made them claw at each other like that, but as I was going to break up the fight there was a loud explosion. That's all I can remember."

The following is said to be a correct but partial list of the names of those of the passengers, officers, and crew of The Merryville Commerce who were killed by the fatal explosion of her boiler.

Crew

John Ivor, first engineer

Jas. Plotsky, second engineer

Mr. Collins, carpenter

Mr. Bradley, a white fireman

Peter ___ , a white French boy, second cook

Mr. Groomsmen, sailor

Mr. Friar, sailor

Five negroes, four of them firemen and the other the steward

Passengers

Nathaniel Parker, Senator, Gloucester County

Albert Hutchins, City of Williamsburg Council Member

Margaret O'Rourke, midwife

Quincy O'Rourke, ten year old boy

Mr. Snyder, an engineer from New Albany

Two brothers named Smith from Delaware

Two brothers named Jessup from the vicinity of Trenton, New Jersey

Mr. Bartlett from Hartford

A French gentleman, whose name is not known

Two passengers who died in the Hospital

The mate of the boat, 2d pilot, and a black fireman remained on board and whose recovery no hopes were entertained.

Bardo:

n., from the Tibetan, meaning transitional state

Margaret

osie met Quincy and me at the gate. She was beautiful, and except for one small star-shaped spot on her right cheek she showed no signs of the scars from the fire that had haunted her life. "I left that there on purpose," she said, when asked by Quincy. "I wanted to be certain I remembered what Albert did. Sometimes the forgiveness overcomes our memories. I want to remember."

Quincy nodded. He had known her in the before times, and they were content together.

"Where's Albert?" he asked finally. Albert was a new soul to him, and his concern touched me greatly.

"He went another way," Josie stated. "He's got a lot of teaching to go through before he goes back."

"So we have to wait for him for however long it takes," Quincy stated.

"Yes, and it may take some time 'cause you know you incarnate all together – the four of you with your connections to each other in past lives. You all have karmic debts to each other."

"Was he here before?"

"Yes. The spirit guides will help him decide on his next life and he will have to agree. He had a hard transition this time. I think he knew what he had done."

"How long before we are together again?"

"Until Albert can look at his last incarnation and say he didn't realize how beautiful humans are. He is endowed with the power to save, redeem and heal himself. He had that before the beginning of the world. Some use their power for good; some for selfish reasons."

"And Nathaniel's soul?" I asked.

"Right here," a familiar voice said behind me.

We settled into the light and peace, the three of us. Why we ever wanted to go back to earthly bodies I could not reckon. We basked in the love of each other and Josie.

And we waited for the soul known as Albert.

Book 3

Margene

"Then I will speak upon the ashes."
Sojourner Truth

July 1915

Quinton Dunn

I had the dream again.

I try to stop it. I do. I know Father will be angry because I am afraid. He yells at Mama when I wake up screaming in the middle of the night. I do try to remember it is just a dream. I try, but the fire is burning me.

Sometimes my mother comes running to hush me. "It's a dream," she says. "Just a dream." Sometimes she hears me first and gets there in time. If Father arrives before her, he pulls her back to bed. I hear him telling her to ignore me. He says it is just a dream. "Stop babying him," he says.

Tonight Mama does not hear me first. Tonight father comes into my room. He sits in the chair by my bed. "You must stop this, Quinton. You are seven years old now. You know this is not real."

Tonight he does not have his slippers on. I look down at the floor – at his withered up foot. It is gray, like a mouse I caught once. Gray and shriveled and small. Like I feel right now. He sees me looking and he pulls his foot back under the chair. "Try to go back to sleep," he says.

He leaves and I stare into the murkiness that surrounds me. It is not as dark as the forest in my dream. Nothing is as black as everything in the forest. I do not want to go back to sleep. I know if I do, the dream will come. I will scream. It is always unchanged.

In the dream, I am playing alone outside. The warm sun is fiery on my naked arms. The breeze drifts through the golden fuzz that sprouts from my skin.

Rusty is with me. He is fetching the sticks I throw for him. He lumbers after them. He used to jump to get them, but now is he too old. One stick goes into the woods. He runs after it, tail billowing behind him. He does not come back right away, so I go in after him.

In the beginning, the woods are not scary, just a little darker than the full sunlight I came from. The sunlight is sifted through trees that are thick with summer leaves. I feel safe. I am not afraid. I hear Rusty barking. He probably found a rabbit. He loves chasing rabbits, even though the rabbit usually wins. I run toward the sound. The further I go into the woods, the shadier it gets, until everything is a black skin that will not let any light through. The air outside this place was moved by a calm breeze; now it is unmoving and I find it hard to breathe.

"Rusty, Rusty – where are you? Come, boy," I am yelling. There is a blue light before me, pulling me into it. Rusty is there, sitting quietly in front of it.

Rusty never sits quietly.

I call him again, but his ears do not move at the sound of his name. All I can see is his back, the hair of his yellow coat as quiet as the rest of him. I move to the side and see the blue light is not a light at all, but a flame.

I remember last year going to the state fair in Richmond. There was a man there with a beautiful silver watch. He invited people onto a stage, and he would swing the watch in front of their faces then have them do silly things. Pretend they were a chicken. Bark like a dog.

Maybe the man is here and found Rusty and is making him pretend to be a statue.

The old-air smell is embracing me, holding me back from Rusty and the flame. But the blue light of the flame breaks that embrace, and I move forward. Toward Rusty. Toward the blue glowing flame. It remains motionless, sticking out in contrast to the dark and cold. I feel like I am confined in a box. I cannot see the sky anymore. In some way, I know it is only the woods I am walking through. I tell myself I can leave at any time. With or without Rusty, I can walk out.

The flame flickers, and from it comes Mama's voice. "Quinnie," she croons. "Come here and get warm with me." It is so dark I cannot see her. Rusty is sitting before the fire, waiting for me. I walk toward my dog and the blue glow. The air smells ancient – not at all like my mother's perfumed skin.

For the first time I am afraid. I want nothing more than to escape and go home. "Rusty," I whisper. "Come on, boy. Let's go." I touch the fur on the back of his head, and it is very hot. I walk in front of him and stand facing him – between him and the blue light – and I see he is melting as if he were made from wax. The two places in his face that once held his warm brown eyes are now black, flaming holes. There is dense smoke pouring from the openings. He makes no sound and I know he will never again chase another stick or rabbit.

This is the part in the dream where I run. But no matter how hard I run, I cannot get out of the forest. I am screaming for Mama. The darkness has become high walls and I am banging into them. There is no way out. I am trapped by the forest.

My back becomes very hot. I look at my arms, and the golden hairs are burning. At first I don't feel any pain, and then suddenly the blue light is all over me. I am burning, my skin is burning and I scream, but nothing comes out of my mouth. I can see the black walls now, like I am in a box with a lid and no way out

Then the wind comes. A hot wind, blowing hard inside the box. The lid of the box burns away, and the wind picks up the fire and sends it out the top. I hear crackling as the trees are covered with a hot cloak. It covers the woods. The green leaves are now brown and gray and shriveled.

I look at the trees and the leaves are covered with small, withered feet – like my father's bad foot. The fire roars to life, scorching and grabbing everything in its path. I hear Mama's voice, "Come here, Quinnie. Don't fear the fire."

The flames turn and I see Father's face glowing red and orange at the top. It turns and flies toward me. I feel its embrace, and it snatches me up with it, and together we climb higher toward the top. Only my father gets out of the box. I stay in the clinch of the flames. My Rusty is gone. My mother is gone. It has taken everything from me - burning me and everything I have ever loved.

I see my father leaning into the box. He is saying to me, "Stop being such a baby. Stop it."

I want to stop screaming, but I cannot. I want the fire to kill me, but it does not. It is a searing that never stops. I try to suck the hot air into my lungs so I will die. I feel pain, hot and burning, and I cannot stop it. And as much as I want to, I cannot die. I keep burning and burning.

Imagine, if you can, the wind suddenly changing, the sparks within the air more dense than any skyrocket that could be shot off in your face, with a temperature that in an instant cooked every exposed part of your body, with only a moment to realize your condition before falling down unconscious, and then, as if this were not enough misfortune, awaken to find your clothes half burned off, crazy with pain. I cannot die. This must be the hell they talk about in Sunday school.

I yell to my father about the fire. He screams back, "There is no fire, Quinton." Then I know no one can see the fire except me.

Quiet. No one screaming. The top of the burning box has a new face; the face of a black woman comes and looks over the edge where my father stood only moment earlier. She climbs down into the box with me. Her cloak is made from green plants and herbs, like Mama has in her special room. She comes to me and I see the plants are not a cloak as I thought, but are living and connected to her somehow. The roots are growing into her brown skin, like she is made of dirt from the earth.

She moves toward me easily, and the flames retreat from her. They are afraid of this black woman covered in earth. The flames lick at her, trying to burn her skin. She is bold in front of the fire, and she keeps coming toward me. I am still burning, but the pain is gone. She comes to me and picks me up. "There, there, child. I will heal you," she says softly. It is my mother's voice coming from her lips.

She holds me to her cool body. We are lifted up together toward the new light from the sun and the fire stops and the pain ends.

Margene Dunn

Quinnie is screaming again. The night terrors, the doctor calls them. I hear him too late – Alfred is already awake and heading down the hallway to his room. I finger the amulet around my neck. The luck ball is safe, hiding in the box buried deep within the ground under the Oak tree. Strange how my husband never sees the amulet around my neck.

My husband is angry – he is walking quickly with the thump-thump that his uneven gait makes on the hardwood floor. I know he is angry, for he did not even take the time to put on his slippers that hide the gray foot.

I force myself not to get up. He will only send me from his room if I do, and Quinnie's screams will last longer as he calls for me. We are prisoners in this house, held captive by a man I do not love, whose one redeeming factor in his life is Quinnie - his heir. Quinnie - the one I sacrificed everything for so the Dunn lineage would continue. My husband, Alfred. A man cursed by his loneliness, his moral poverty, and his need to be loved by his father. I wonder what his soul is like - will it wander after it leaves his body in death? Does he even have a soul - this man who shares my bed?

I pray for Kassie to go to my son in his dream. I pray for her intervention. She can stop his tears. He tells me of the black woman with the plants who picks him up from the flames in the furnace, and holds him and cures him. I know it is my Kassie, for I see her in my dreams. She is leading us toward Nathan and wrapping us three together with her cloak. In my dream, we are with Nathan forever, Quinnie and I, and Kassie hovers above us protecting us from the wrath of Alfred Dunn.

Kassie has been long dead, killed by those who believed she was a witch. Her herbal teachings lived on in my mother, passed on to me and now I pass them to my son. No one can break that connection – not on the earth or in the heavens.

Alfred Dunn

In my hurriedness I forgot my slippers again. I know my foot frightens Quinton. Margene will not even sleep in my bed unless it is covered with a sock or two. It is my burden that I am required to carry in this life. It kept me from father's favor, as a military career was out of the question. He built a shrine to my younger brother Cam, killed during the tornado on May 10, 1905, in Snyder, Oklahoma. Cam and his pregnant bride Suzanne were visiting her family. Both died in the storm. He took the shrine down when Quinton was born. I finally gained my father's favor the day I gave him an heir.

Growing up, Mother comforted me, but she could never replace father's lack of interest. He tolerated me – the last of his line (or so he thought) because of his conviction I was unqualified for military service and much else in his eyes. "No woman will want you, Alfred," he said to me many times.

Then Margene became my wife in the summer of 1907. He arranged our marriage as a business deal with her father. My father held the bill of debt on her father's steam boat that ran between Baltimore, Maryland and Norfolk, Virginia. Margene's father had four young mouths to feed and a sickly wife, and Father knew of the feisty, beautiful and strong willed Margene. She was a nurse at the Memorial Hospital at Twelfth and Broad Streets in Richmond and kept company with one Nathan Hollister, a political foe of ours who sought her favors. He came from poor kinfolk and could not offer her the power and prestige I could.

Father found her intriguing. She was of sturdy Irish stock, hazel eyes and long, brown curly hair. She was full breasted, with a freckled pug nose and melodious laugh. Father had me visit the hospital and meet her to see if a union would be acceptable. It was the only time he ever ventured to ask my opinion about anything that concerned me.

I told father I found her acceptable.

And so the negotiations began. Father spoke to Captain O'Donnell, Margene's father who owned the Margie Belle, and offered him forgiveness of all his debts in exchange for his daughter.

"You realize you are asking me to sell my daughter to you," Captain O'Donnell is reported to have said. My father merely nodded, and the deal was done.

June, 1905

Nathan Hollister

"Margene! What an unusual name."

Those were the first words I ever spoke to her. She was 21 years old, smart, beautiful in her starched white apron tied in a perky bow. It covered her nurse's uniform, the long sleeves pushed up to her elbows revealing the rosy flesh of her forearms. Her nurse's cap was attempting to control her brown curly hair, harnessing its wildness. A strand had escaped and hung down her back. How I want to pull that cap from her head, release that mound of hair, kiss those lips… I felt feeble. Apparently it showed.

"Mr. Hollister? Are you all right?" she asked.

"No. I have just met the Goddess Athena… or are you Venus?"

The Nursing Supervisor walked by at that moment, made a snorting sound that avowed her disapproval. Margene turned bright red. "Mr. Hollister. Kindly refrain from such comments."

"Yes ma'am," I responded.

As soon as her supervisor was out of earshot, I asked Margene for a date for dinner. She said no. I kept coming back until, three weeks later, she accepted. After that first date, she kept turning me away.

I was in love the first time I saw her bite into the meal we were served at the Harrison Supper Club on Broad Street. It took her a little longer. Eight months longer.

I was poor. My family on both sides were abolitionists who moved to Virginia during Reconstruction. They were a part of the Freedmen's Bureau, which started operations in 1865 to assist the vast numbers of recently emancipated slaves. My father was from Vermont. He met and married my Connecticut-born and reared mother here in Virginia. She had come to teach the newly freed slave children who had been prohibited from education and attaining literacy. Unlike our counterparts who came to the South to exploit the chaotic situation for personal gain, we came with good intentions. My father finally had to admit the road to hell was paved with good intentions.

Forty years later good intentions were meaningless. We will always be carpetbaggers in the minds of these ignorant fools. These Richmonders always wanted to know my lineage, my mother's maiden name, where I was from, or who my people were. I spoke with a Southern accent and no one who didn't know my 'people' would have ever guessed I was a Yankee Northerner. Y'all or not, I grew up wanting to change the South.

My mother came here to teach, my father to serve in the Virginia Congress and use his experience with the northern railroad to rebuild the system destroyed during the war. My family came to Virginia to reform her, and she destroyed us – refusing us credit, a place to live, burning our home to the ground. My parents, fearing for their lives, returned to Vermont. I stayed. I thought I could change things.

"You're a smart boy," one of the Jim Crow leaders told me. "But you're a smart ass, too." He laughed, slapped me on the back, then had his henchmen break the fingers on my right hand. It didn't stop me, the roughing up – I just learned to use my left hand instead.

White Democrats regained power in 1890. My parents were careful to keep me educated at a very early age about local and national politics. I paid attention, and later followed the Democrats, resolute to stop the passage of their laws establishing racial segregation in public facilities. I sat in on their 1901 constitutional convention, determined to have my voice heard when they were focused on restricting black voting rights without violating the Fifteenth Amendment to the United States Constitution or disenfranchising poor whites. They created their poll taxes and literacy tests – unless you were a veteran who fought on behalf of the Confederacy, in which case you were grandfathered in. The schools my mother had fought for disappeared; they enforced segregation laws and abolished the county court systems. They did all of this without ratification by the electorate. I posted flyers everywhere, handed them out on street corners, stood in front of the state capitol and talked with anyone who would listen. I was beaten for my efforts, spit on, and demonized. But I did not stop. Still, they did not listen to my voice.

Despite all this consternation, I stayed. This particular day, as I was carried into the Memorial

Hospital in Richmond after my latest beating, I was seriously rethinking my position.

Then I met Margene. Nothing was the same after that.

Margene O'Donnell

Nathan will tell you it was love at first sight for him. It was not for me. I thought him quite full of himself, a talker, a braggart. He caused me great harm with the Nursing Director at my place of employment. Nurses were supposed to be chaste, and the first words he spoke to me were those of a lover. Our Director, a foul heifer who delighted in writing up demerits for the hard-working nurses under her control, was quite uncompromising. She had a multitude of signs that read: *Any nurse who smokes, uses liquor in any form, gets her hair done at a beauty shop, or frequents dance halls will give the Director of Nurses good reason to suspect her worth, intentions, and integrity.*

That sign didn't stop me from engaging in ALL of those forbidden activities, for the doctors and staff liked me… and hated the heifer, whose ugly sister reputation led to the rumor she was a relative of someone important, otherwise she would have never had the job. She used to point to her scaly lips and proclaim, "These lips will never touch tobacco or liquor." Or much else, I thought.

It also helped that Mr. Cameron Dunn, a member of the board of directors of our esteemed hospital, had given a good report on my skills during a recent trip to my area. He had even brought his son, Alfred, to meet me. Alfred was a sad man who was under the shadow of his revered father. He had a pronounced limp. Someone said his nickname was 'mouse foot', or something on that order. Father and son spoke with me for a few minutes. I felt as if Alfred were sizing me up for a casket. The heifer saw this conversation and was duly impressed. Even if she had not been impressed, I would still do as I pleased. The heifer considered me irredeemable, a wild child; I considered her a withered up old crone.

Nevertheless, I was a dedicated nurse, not looking for romance or anything to take me from my career. A man, especially a man like Nathan Hollister, was the farthest thing from my thoughts. I was very interested in the suffrage movement and what I believed was the unchaining of women – not just in the voting booth, but in the boudoir. We were hearing rumors about European women bobbing their hair.

No, I was not looking, nor did I need a man in my life. I must admit, however, that from the day Nathan Hollister darkened my doorstep until the day the good Lord would call me home, he was never out of my thoughts.

I did not let him know how I felt for the longest time. Our love affair began slowly. He would push for date after date, I would say no. He made me laugh, blush, stutter. I made him crazy. He had a reputation as a rounder, and women literally swooned at his feet – to hear him tell it. I had a reputation as a dedicated nurse who didn't cotton to such malarkey. He would touch my arm whilst looking into my eyes; I would pull back. He would take my elbow when we walked; I would pull away. This cat and mouse game went on for months. He even went so far as to let me see him in the company of other woman, flaunting them before me on the street. He admitted to waiting until he knew I would be walking home, and then would escort some lovely woman – walking toward me, chatting and laughing. I learned later it was his cousins who were in on the conspiracy to break down my resolve.

I decided he wasn't for me. After all, if he could flit from one flower to another, how could I expect him to love me as a husband should, treat me as an equal, be my rock in hard times? I began turning him down for dinner. I walked a different way home so as not to run into him. If he came into the hospital, and required care from one of his recent altercations, I would ask another of my fellow nurses to tend to him. "You are all he talks about. It as if he injected himself with a Victrola needle the way he plays on and on about you," they would report. I turned away so they would not see the tears appearing in my eyes.

I had been to the grocers on a Saturday afternoon about eight months after we first met. I was headed back to my room at Mrs. Hudgins' Boarding House, not far from the hospital. I wanted some Irish butter and clotted cream to go with my scones on Sunday morning before heading off for church. It was a beautiful day, the sapphire sky dotted with puffs of white. The grocer Davidson had given me some Seville oranges for the other nurses at the boarding house. "For all their hard work," he said. I was content with my small parcel, enjoying the autumn afternoon and grateful for being away from the hospital and all its drama. I turned the corner and my way was blocked by Nathan Hollister holding the hugest bunch of flowers I had ever seen. "What… ," I managed.

"That is my question, Margene O'Donnell. What is wrong with me that you won't even give me the time of day? Was our one and only dinner so repulsive? Did I have food in my teeth? Was I boorish?" He grinned at me.

"I want nothing to do with you, thank you very much Mr. Hollister. Please stand aside and let me pass or I shall summon a policeman and have you arrested."

"I will step aside on one condition. You will tell me why you are so repulsed by me."

"I want nothing to do with you. You are a rogue and a scalawag. You always have a woman on your arm. You have no need of me. You have plenty of company! Besides, sir, you would simply break my heart and leave me thrashing on the floor. I know your type."

Actually, I didn't know his type. Furthermore, I blurted out the last part never intending to let him know I had feelings for him. I was so annoyed with myself, and since he wasn't moving, I pushed him. He fell backward, splitting his pants in the process. The flowers fell into the street and were run over by the next passing vehicle. I began to laugh.

Nathan jumped to his feet, his dignity and pride lying in the street with the flowers. His face was changed, anger replacing his teasing confidence displayed earlier. "You win, Miss O'Donnell. I shall not bother you again."

He turned to walk away, his white union suit hanging from the split in the rear of his trousers, resembling the tail of a bunny. I was bent over laughing. He turned, walked rapidly toward me, pinned my arms by my sides and kissed me. Full on the mouth.

Then he walked away.

I ran after him, grabbing his flapping undergarments protruding from the split in his breeches, in order to stop him. He turned, tears in his eyes. "I cannot help it, Margene. I love you. You don't want me and I cannot change that. My heart is shattered. I do not want to live."

"Let's get you home – you have your drawers hanging out here, flapping in the breeze," I said. "Where do you live?"

"My cottage is just around the corner, on Floyd."

"Come, then. I'll go with you and we'll have some tea. Here," I handed him the sack of Seville oranges, "carry this behind you."

Off we went, him carrying the sack to cover his buttocks and preserve his dignity and me laughing all the way.

Despite my mirth, I had the oddest sensation of being watched the entire time.

Alfred Dunn

I went to Father that afternoon. Watching her laugh and run the streets with Nathan Hollister made me believe that time was of the essence. I told him I wanted to make Margene my wife, and that I felt she would be more than suitable to carry on the family name. I did not reveal the encounter on the street between my bride-to-be and that failure, Nathan Hollister. I was afraid he might consider her spoiled goods, kissing a man full on the mouth in broad daylight.

Father and I discussed the courtship timetable and how we would make certain her father was in agreement. "Should I go to him and ask for her hand?" I questioned.

"No, I don't think that will be necessary, Alfred. I believe Captain O'Donnell will inform his daughter of the arrangement once I have spoken to him. Let me take some time to formulate the agreement and then arrange to talk with him. I must say, Alfred, I am delighted at your decision, and look forward to the grandson you and Margene will produce to carry on our name."

That was the first time Father had praised me. I wasn't certain how to proceed, so I asked, "What should I do now? Ask her to dinner?"

"No, that isn't necessary. Let me speak to the good Captain first, and we'll move on from there. As I said, it will take some time for me to put this all together for everyone's mutual benefit."

I was dismissed, and went up to my room to contemplate my life as Margene's husband.

Nathan Hollister

I was mortified. I could feel the wind blowing through the split in my britches. Margene's laughter didn't help.

We were headed back to my small cottage on Floyd Avenue. For tea.

I hoped I had tea.

I opened the front door and ushered her inside. If my nosy neighbors asked, I would simply tell them she was one of my female cousins. I took her wrap and hung it on the hook in the foyer.

"Please, come in," I said.

"Nice," she responded. "I do love these quaint houses. Do you live here alone?"

"Yes. It was our family home before my parents went back to Vermont. Actually, this is our second family home. Our first was burned to the ground by people who didn't like us. They called us carpetbaggers."

She was speechless, covering her mouth with her right hand. "I am so sorry. Were you a part of the Reconstruction movement?"

"My parents were. It was a bit before my time. My mother came here to teach the children of the slaves. My father was in the state Senate and helped rebuild the railroad. But, things changed... "

She was quiet, looking at the various books lying around on my somewhat dusty shelves. She picked up one book. It was a collection of essays by Emmeline Pankhurst.

"Would you like to go to a meeting with me tonight?" she asked.

"What type of meeting?"

"A group of women who meet in secret with others. They call themselves the National American Woman Suffrage Association. We're working toward a constitutional amendment to secure the right to vote for women."

I looked at her. "Suffragette's meeting?"

"Yes, and there are men who have joined our ranks. Well, do you want to go with me or not?"

"I'm not sure I have another pair of suitable trousers."

"Well, get out of those and let me mend them... unless you are using your split britches as an excuse not to attend."

I stripped right in front of her, handed her my trousers, and found a needle and thread. She sat chatting with me in my union suit as if it were the most natural thing in the world. When she was finished, she rummaged around in the kitchen and fixed tea. She sat it on the small table in front of the sofa and sat next to me.

"Nathan," she began. "I have strong feelings for you. I need to get to know you on a different level to know if we can grow side by side. I am not traditional partner material. I am my own person, stubborn and headstrong. I need to know you before I tell you I love you. I am uncertain exactly what your intentions are, and I am not one to enter into a partnership or union of any sort where I am not at least on an equal footing with the other party. Do you understand?"

"I do," I muttered.

"Now, if your intentions are to simply take away my virginity in your bed and then move on to some other conquest, then you'd best tell me now."

"I want to marry you, if you'll have me. We'll be poor as church mice, but I will be your undying champion. Better, worse, all that other rubbish. I will take very good care of you, Margene. I promise. I swear to God."

She stood, bent and kissed me full on the lips. She pulled me to my feet, clasped my hand, and walked with me into the bedroom, where we made love over and over again until it was time for the Suffragette meeting.

August 15, 1907

Margene O'Donnell

Papa surprised me this afternoon at the hospital. My work schedule did not allow for trips home, so I haven't seen him or my Mum for months. He and my four younger siblings live in Baltimore on Light Street near the steamboat terminals. They were fortunate to have avoided the Great Baltimore Fire in 1904, and the rebuilt terminal was a vast improvement over the old one. The rats, however, were the same.

The *Old Bay Line* based in Baltimore had given him a run for his money. He could not keep up with the luxury steamboats that ferried passengers and cargo on the Chesapeake, and had opted to carry fewer passengers and more cargo. Cargo transport had boomed during the Reconstruction period after the War Between the States, and competition grew fearsome as more and more men cast their hat into the ring.

Papa had managed to hold on, but he was deeply in debt. Cameron Dunn had lent him money to, as he put it, 'stay afloat'. Cargo traffic had increased in the past six months, but supporting my four younger siblings and my Mum, who was recently diagnosed with consumption, was an arduous task. He was gone a good deal of the time, forcing the eldest at home to quit school and take care of the family. At thirteen years of age, she was in charge. I sent them part of my wages each month, but the paltry fifteen dollars I sent was hardly enough to keep them in food. Fortunately, I was a mouth they did not have to feed.

He had taken a side trip to Richmond on this voyage. It was the first time I ever remember him fluctuating from his normal Baltimore to Norfolk route. He hugged me tightly and whispered that we needed to talk. "Is something wrong with Mum or the children?" I asked, unable to mask the fear in my voice.

"No, they are fine. We just need to talk."

I was off that evening at 8 p.m. Nathan had other plans, and it was just as well, for I wanted to disclose the news about him to Papa gently. I wasn't certain how he would take to his new son-in-law. They were very different, although somewhat on the same side politically. Nonetheless, I know my father was hoping for a physician in the family – not a poor rabble-rouser.

Sharply at 8 p.m., Papa was waiting outside the entrance to the hospital. He held our wrapped up dinner under his arm. It was from a fancy restaurant around the corner. "I visited them earlier, and asked them to package something for a celebration," he said when I asked about the treat. I was starving, and I could smell the roast beef coming from the package he held tightly while we walked the short distance to my boardinghouse. Mrs. Hudgins was ever vigilant to ensure the virtue of her girls. As we came in through the massive glass and wood front door, she jumped out from behind a pillar. She had probably been watching us walk up the sidewalk to her front door. "And who might this be?" she barked.

"Mrs. Hudgins, this is my father, Captain O'Donnell. Papa, Mrs. Hudgins. She owns the boardinghouse."

Papa removed his hat and bowed. Mrs. Hudgins, obviously charmed if the blush to her otherwise sallow complexion was any indication, took his hand and shook it. "Pleasure," she said.

"Papa and I are going to use the main dining room and eat our dinner together. He is up from Baltimore for the evening, and will be leaving at around 10:00 p.m., if that is acceptable," I said.

"Oh, yes. Yes, of course. Just no men upstairs," she tittered, motioning us on.

"I am glad you are in such good hands," Papa remarked, loud enough for Mrs. Hudgins to catch every word.

We sat and ate and chatted. Papa pushed his food around, while I devoured everything in sight. I had to loosen the ties on my apron when I was finished. I leaned back, closed my eyes and sighed. "Wonderful, Papa, just wonderful. Thank you."

He took both of my hands in his, and when I opened my eyes I saw tears running down his cheeks. I had never, ever in my entire life seen my father weep. Never.

I sat straight up in my chair. "Papa, what is it?"

"I have something to discuss with you," he finally managed. "It involves your future as a wife and the future of our family's survival."

The first person who darted into my head was Nathan. I was astounded that he knew about my beloved, as I hadn't mentioned a word. I had hoped to have two days off at the end of this month to take Nathan home to meet the family. Knowing them, it was best to spring things on the group rather than be subtle. "And I have something very important to tell you to, Papa! I have met…"

"Please, let me get through this," he began. "Just hear me out, daughter. When I have told you all, then we can talk."

I nodded.

"My darling Margene, you know how terribly hard times are right now, for me and for the shipping business. Your poor mama has been ill for months, and with the children at home it has been very difficult. Business will change at some point, but I have had to borrow a great deal of money. The individual who holds that note has come to me and demanded repayment. Even though he is a very rich man, it is an investment, and he does have the right to receive payment on his investment with me. So, he has proposed a business deal…"

Papa stopped at this time and wiped his eyes. I had never seen Papa cry, not even when my youngest sister died three days after she was born. I remember him holding her tiny lifeless body, kissing her on the forehead, handing her back to my mother and walking from the room.

I placed my hands over his, looked at his grieving face and said, "Papa, what is it? How can I help?"

"Oh my God, Margene, no father should ever have to ask his daughter what I'm about to ask you. You have met Alfred Dunn, is that correct?"

"Yes, Papa. His father is a very important person on the board of the hospital where I work. He brought his son Alfred around the other day and introduced me. He seems to be a very sad young man. I noticed he had a terrible limp. Was it the result of an injury in the war?"

"No, he was not in the war. It is a deformity. He nearly lost his foot to an infection as a child because of the work of a black slave woman who was an herbalist. She saved his foot, but it became deformed due to the wrapping and length of time the medication was required. Some people call this 'mouse foot'."

"Oh, how sad for him. Is he his father's only son?"

"No, he had an older brother who distinguished himself in the war, but he and his wife were killed in the fire in Oklahoma when they went to visit her family with their young son. Alfred is all he has left."

"Oh Papa, how tragic that is! How very sad. I feel so badly for Alfred and for his father. But what does this have to do with me?"

Papa pulled his hands away and placed them in his lap. I looked at them and they were shaking. He was trying to control it, but he couldn't. "Margene, as you can imagine, it is very difficult for Alfred to find a suitable mate due to his physical problems. And his father longs for a male heir to his fortune. And that is why he has asked for your hand in marriage. This arrangement will nullify my debt to him, and an arrangement has been made to take care of your mother and the rest of the children should something happen to him or me. This money has been put in a trust and cannot be touched by anyone but your mother and the children. In addition, you will be well provided for. For the rest of your life. Alfred's father has assured me that is the case. I have met with his attorneys, and they are drawing up the paperwork now. Unfortunately, all of these decisions and the ramifications rest on your shoulders."

I studied his face, his white, well-trimmed beard, his blue eyes, and his mane of white hair that ended just at his shoulders. I searched his eyes for an answer. Surely my father was not selling me into an arranged marriage to cover the family debt.

"No, Papa! Please don't ask this of me. You know I love you, I love mama, I love my brothers and sisters, but I cannot marry this man! I don't love him! I will never love him. I was so excited to see you tonight because I wanted to take you over and introduce you to the man that I do love, the man who holds all my hopes and dreams... please! Please, Papa. I must tell you I cannot do this. I don't love this man. You told me to always marry for love! Please, listen to me. I cannot marry Alfred Dunn."

He said nothing. He stared down at his shaking hands in his lap. Finally, he raised his eyes to my face. I had seen that look only once before when I was on the paddleboat with him, and we went through a very dangerous part of the river. He was totally focused on the journey ahead, with no regard for anything but getting through this particular part without running aground.

Finally, he said, "I'm sorry. You have no choice. We all must make our sacrifices in this life, and this one is yours. I will make the necessary arrangements, and Alfred's father will come 'round for you tomorrow morning to pick you up and carry you to their home. Your mother and the children are coming up for the weekend. It will be a small wedding at their family estate. The arrangements with your superiors are being made as we speak. After the wedding, a brief honeymoon is planned, and you will not being going back to the hospital, but will go to your new home in Deltaville, Virginia."

I stood up, raising my right fist. I was convulsing with the anger that had been building throughout his entire explanation of how the rest of my life would play out. "No," I screamed in his face, inching closer and closer to him until our noses almost touched. "No, I will not. You cannot sell me like some slave. No!"

And he slapped me. For the first time in my life, he slapped my face hard with his right hand, with all his might, knocking me backwards into my chair. He stood, pushing the chair back, and picked up his hat from the floor where it had fallen. "No more discussion, Margene. Your last day at the hospital was today. Your things have been retrieved, and tomorrow Mr. Dunn and Alfred will come here with a servant and get the rest. No more discussion."

And he left. I ran after him, but it was too late. I ran down the road in the freezing rain to Nathan's house, banging on the door with all my capacity, screaming his name. I heard him fumbling with the lock and I fell inside when the door swung open.

I told him the whole story, how I was being sold for a debt, like a brood mare. He held me and rocked me, knowing full well that the situation was hopeless, and short of running off and ruining my family, I had no choice. Tomorrow I would marry Alfred Dunn.

August 17, 1907

Margene O'Donnell Dunn

At 2:30 in the afternoon, on an unusually warm Saturday, I became Alfred Dunn's wife. My entire family came on the steamboat from Baltimore. My mother helped me dress in the gown provided by the Dunn family. She cried the entire time. Just before the wedding, she gave me the luck ball and amulet passed on to her by Kassie. "Put this on later, it will keep you safe," she said between sobs. Safe from what, I thought! Could it be any worse than this moment? My brothers and sisters were my attendants. "Do we call you Uncle Alfie?" the youngest asked.

"Yes, that would be quite nice," Alfred responded, scooping her up in his arms. He was having a grand old time. That got everyone but me into the spirit.

Mr. and Mrs. Cameron Dunn had flowers, and Bishop Prescott of the Presbyterian Church blessed our marriage. My father offered his arm to walk me into the parlor where the ceremony would take place; but I refused, instead taking Alfred's arm. Together we walked into the midst of the small gathering.

It took less than fifteen minutes for me to become Mrs. Dunn. We had a nice reception afterwards, with lovely food and drink. At around 5 p.m., Alfred and I left for our brief honeymoon in Virginia Beach, where we stayed at the Virginia Beach Hotel on the boardwalk.

The hotel was lovely. It was built in 1883, and had such modern amenities as gas lighting and indoor lavatories. At first, I felt out of place in the three-story luxury hotel, but the wardrobe Mrs. Dunn had purchased for me on the day before the wedding made things easier. I fit in with the affluent clientele who traveled to Virginia Beach for the fresh air and saltwater, thought by some to be medically beneficial.

I decided to manipulate the situation to my advantage. I knew it was hopeless to fight against my father's plans, so my only available course of action was to go along with them and get from the Dunn family what I could in the way of money and security. Hopefully I would be able to save enough so I might run away and join my beloved Nathan.

The honeymoon night was horrid! I was used to Nathan's passionate lovemaking. Alfred kept his mouse foot covered with a wrapping. Fortunately, it was over quickly and he fell right to sleep. I endured four more episodes the week we were in Virginia Beach.

We returned to Richmond to spend the next two days with Alfred's family. Jessie, the daughter of the herbalist who had saved Alfred's foot when it became infected as a child, was assigned to come with us to Deltaville as my housekeeper and companion.

Mr. Dunn had purchased a car for me. Jessie knew how to drive, which was unusual as most of the negra women had little access to vehicles, let alone driving lessons. However, Mrs. Dunn was deathly afraid of the automobile, so Jessie learned to operate it in order to transport her to various appointments.

The house in Deltaville was at the end of a lane, a large, two-story structure that looked out over the Chesapeake Bay.

"Do you want me to carry you over the threshold?" Alfred asked.

"No, I'll walk," I said. "After all, you're the one who has to drive back to Richmond tonight."

Jessie was behind Alfred, carrying the bags. It took her three trips to bring everything into the house.

"Oh, the view," I cried, running to the windows along the eastern wall of the house. "It looks like I could touch the waves."

"Yes," Alfred responded, walking up behind me and placing his hands on my shoulders. "This house has been my family's summer cottage for many years. It has all the modern conveniences, even an indoor toilet, which is a rarity in these parts!"

It was furnished with lovely things and had three bedrooms, a huge kitchen, and gas lights. "The telephone isn't like the ones in Richmond," Alfred added. "We have an operator who places calls for you. This is one of the only telephones in the area," he said proudly. "Father knew I would be gone a great deal of the time, so he insisted one be put in."

"What 'bout the groceries, Mr. Alfred?" Jessie questioned. "There ain't no stores for miles 'round here, and I think we would eat up all the stuff we brought from Richmond."

"Yes, a purveyor will drive in three days a week. I think Father is using the fellow you recommended,

Margene. You just give him a list when he is here, and everything will be delivered on the next trip. All paid for, by the way."

I don't know why he had to add the 'all paid for' part, but it was just as well.

"Anything?" Jessie asked, her eyes darting from the boxes of food she had carted into the kitchen.

"Yes. Why, did you have something specific in mind, Jessie?" Alfred asked.

"Strawberries. I always wants to eat strawberries in December."

"Even strawberries in December are no problem," Alfred said as he led us upstairs for a tour of the rest of the house.

I began to realize that if you had enough money, anything was possible.

Jessie and I settled in for the winter. Alfred stayed in Richmond, visiting two or three times a month. He was very involved with his father, who suddenly had taken a liking to his son now that he was married.

On our honeymoon, Alfred had confessed to me that he was an afterthought in his father's life. Convinced he would never amount to anything, never marry, and never have children, Alfred realized he had become a burden. Now that he was married and the possibility of a child was forthcoming, he suddenly had new status in his father's eyes. I understood, because obviously I was a commodity to my own father, something to be traded for the prosperity of his sacred steamboat business. Oh, how I hoped that vessel caught fire and father burned with it.

By December it was quite cold, and I was very ill. I was certain it was the loneliness and separation from Nathan, but Jessie thought otherwise. She contacted Mr. Cameron Dunn, and soon a livery was sent for us. I was admitted to the hospital, very ill indeed. I had lost a great deal of weight in the two months since the wedding, and the doctors feared I had consumption since my lungs appeared to be affected. Mr. Dunn made arrangements for my family to come to the hospital, as the doctors believed I was dying. I refused to see my father, but welcomed everyone else, even though I could only wave through the window from my bed in the isolation unit. I spoke to my visitors through a tube apparatus, and my mother cried without ceasing during the whole ordeal.

On Christmas Day I ate broth with some toast for the first time in sixteen days. My strength began to return, and soon I was eating anything handed to me. The doctors were discussing a surgical intervention, including the pneumothorax or plombage technique which would collapse my infected lung to 'rest' it and allow the lesions to heal. I was familiar with the technique, having assisted in two successful interventions while working as a nurse.

My weight gain surprised the doctors, and soon I was well enough to walk around the tiny isolation room to get some exercise. Doctor Harris was attending me, and during one visit he called in a specialist... not for my lungs! The physician, a Dr. Montgomery who was head of the obstetrics department, came into my room, examined me, and announced that I was pregnant. Learning the consumption diagnosis was an error gave me great relief. I was removed from isolation and placed in a private room with plans to move me to the Dunn house in Richmond, where I would stay until the baby was delivered. Jessie and two other members of the staff traveled to Deltaville to close up the house for the winter and return to Richmond for the duration.

Cameron Dunn was overwhelmed with the news of a pending heir. Alfred was elevated to prince-ship. I had daily visits from Dr. Montgomery, absolutely anything I wanted to eat or drink, and I could do nothing wrong.

On May 24, 1908, I delivered into this world Quinton Cameron Dunn, a healthy eight pound, nine ounce baby boy, the heir Cameron Dunn had believed would never materialize. He held the child before I did, kissing his face and then handing him to Alfred. I was exhausted after the eleven hours of labor, and consented to a wet nurse for the first few days until I regained my strength.

After that, I never let my son out of my sight. My mother came to spend a few days with us and pleaded with me to allow my father to see his grandson. I refused. I wanted nothing to do with Captain O'Donnell.

Alfred Dunn

A son! I have a son! Father held him first, kissed his shiny forehead! There were tears in his eyes, tears which fell upon Quinton's face. Quinton – named for my great-grandfather. Cameron, as his middle name – named for father. "Don't you want to name him Alfred?" he had asked me. "No, father – I want to name him after you."

Margene is exhausted, too tired to put the baby to her breast. We have a nurse coming anyway, at father's insistence. "Let her rest," he said, placing his hand on my shoulder. "She is of sturdy Irish stock, but

I can see where this has drained her. Give her a day or two."

"Margene," he said to my wife, sitting on the side of her bed and placing his hands over hers. "Margene, I hope you can hear me. I am so grateful to you for this beautiful Dunn boy. He is so beautiful, so robust, and so full of life. I will always be indebted to you, my dear. I know this life is not what you would have chosen, but rest assured I will make provisions for you for the rest of your life. Thanks be to God, and to you."

With that he stood and left the room. I watched Margene sleep for a while before heading into father's study.

"What did you mean by that, Father?"

"What, Alfred? Here, have a cigar. You've earned it."

"Earned it? I did nothing!"

"Yes, my son. You gave her your seed and carried on our lineage. You did all you needed to do."

"But what did you mean by 'not the life you would have chosen'?"

He turned, looking out the window at the lawn. "Nothing," he finally said.

"I know you meant something. It was the first words you said to my wife after she gave birth to your grandchild. What did you mean?"

He turned and looked at me, his eyes changing to the color of cold steel. I knew he was angry with my questioning. I did not care. This time I did not back down. "What did you mean?" I asked again.

"I will tell you this, Alfred. Remember it well. The Irish are stupid, lazy people. The English were right during the famines in not feeding and catering to them. They can be bought and sold just like a nigger slave. Sir Charles Trevelyan, a family friend and a British patriot, was right. The judgment of God sent the calamity to teach the Irish a lesson. The Irish did not respond to the free market that would have provided their food. Even those who owned a quarter acre of land expected help from the government. They needed to get up off their lazy asses and get to work and feed themselves."

"But father, she is my wife."

"She is the mother of your heir. She is an Irishwoman first, and Dunn second. Bought and paid for."

With that, he stubbed out his cigar and left the room.

Margene Dunn

I can feel my bones. I ache from delivering this child into the world. Quinton Cameron Dunn. The nurse brought him to me despite Father Dunn's orders otherwise. She said Alfred has approved it over his father's orders. I am holding him now. "I love you, Quinnie. Nothing would ever be more important to me than your birth this day."

The nurse came into the room after a half hour. "I'll take him now, Mrs. Dunn. Mr. Alfred said you are to have your rest and anything else you desire. Ring this bell I have placed on the bedside table if there is anything that you require. Mr. Alfred will visit you later, after you have rested."

I went to sleep immediately, and Kassie and Mama appeared to me in a dream. Kassie had covered her dress with a cape made from bark and herbs. I could see the rope burn on her neck where they had hanged her as a witch because she practiced the slave medicine ways. I was ten years old when she died, hung from a tree by the Klan. She had been teaching me the 'ways' as she called it, the medicines and potions she had passed on to Mama. "You did good, child. He is a beautiful boy," Kassie was saying. I felt so loved at that moment.

I saw myself in the dream rising from my bed and meeting them in the air. We hugged, and then Mama left us. "I am still here in this life for you, Margene. But Kassie must talk with you, and it is best I do not know what she will tell you so no one can force it from me."

Kassie wrapped me in her green bark cloak and hugged me to her body. "There is a fire a'comin," she said. "It is your fire, the one that burns deep within you. It will involve you and other women. Lots of women. You will need help, and you will have it in Jessie."

Another woman appeared in the dream. She looked similar to Kassie, but her cloak was covered in red flowers. "This is Prissy, who was in life Jessie's mama. She is the one who saved your husband Alfred's foot. Go to Jessie, Margene. Trust her. Hear her story."

With those final words Kassie was gone. I was back on the bed in my dream. I fell into an even a deeper sleep, and when I awoke Alfred was sitting in the chair by my bedside.

June, 1908

Nathan Hollister

The newspapers have run pictures of Alfred Dunn and his father Cameron with his newly minted grandson. There is little mention of Margene other than her appropriate role as wife and brood mare.

I saw her yesterday when I delivered the provisions to the Dunn household. It had been her brilliant idea when she came crying to tell me of the forced nuptials. She spoke of the house in Deltaville, and of the limited available resources. After the wedding, she gave Mr. Cameron Dunn my name as a reliable purveyor. Of course she altered my name, just as I altered my appearance with a heavy beard and glasses.

And so we saw each other three times a week for her duration in Deltaville, and then at least weekly during her confinement in Richmond. I was the one who drove the livery taking her from Deltaville to Richmond when she was so ill. It was Jessie, dear, beloved Jessie, who carried our letters back and forth under what would certainly been penalty of death should she have been found out.

Alfred was climbing the ranks of the Democratic Party, his way paved by the money his father threw at his constituents. Both Cameron and Alfred spent weeks in New York helping to reorganize the New York State Association Opposed to Woman Suffrage that had been around since 1897. As a result, there were now over 90 members, and it was Cameron's money that produced pamphlets and publications explaining their views of women's suffrage.

I had gone to suffragette meetings with Margene at a rate of three times per week. They had asked me to speak, and I outlined to them the fact that serious opposition to suffrage was financed by men like Cameron Dunn, who had obtained financing from the whiskey interests and the cotton mill owners of New England and the South. With suffrage tied somewhat to the Temperance movement, the whiskey barons worried that whiskey traffic would be inhibited. The suffrage agenda was also concerned about child labor. Of course the cotton mill owners wanted to maintain child labor, as well as the insufficiently paid labor of women in their mills.

These meetings were often boisterous and very well attended. Guards made certain undesirable elements were not admitted. They feared the anti-suffrage crusade. The anti-suffrage crusade was a cohesive movement that had unified diverse groups with different agendas in the United States. Reconstruction had failed miserably, replaced by a new constitution that forced poll taxes and literacy tests, ensuring the blacks and the poor would be sitting out the elections.

The suffrage campaign in Richmond was knotted up over racial lines. Many whites were loath to allow black women the vote. The base of the suffrage campaign was middle class and white people, and many believed that allowing black women into their ranks would poison the entire movement. There was also a split among the membership over property ownership and states' rights.

Virginia provided such a battlefield, and Cameron and Alfred Dunn took full advantage of this controversy. I heard reports about the activities of the

Dunn family; reports that made my blood boil. They joined with Valencia and Winifred Hale, sisters who changed their names to disguise their identities and presented themselves as leading suffragists. The sisters, like many others, wanted to preserve white supremacy and systematic discrimination against people of color, even while they promoted the rights of women. It was about the rights of white women only.

"So what exactly is it," one woman rose and asked me at a meeting, "that they fear from us?"

"They fear," I responded, "that you will make good on your promises to use the vote for reform measures. And those reform measures will, in effect, change their world."

Shortly after Quinton's birth, Cameron and Alfred left for a tour of southern cities to proclaim their views against the women's vote initiative. They were to be gone for three months, traveling by private railroad car, and accompanied by five servants, including a cook. Rumor had it that prostitutes followed along, with Cameron caught in several compromising situations.

When Margene had fully recovered from her childbirth ordeal, she would get out for an airing at least once a week. Jessie would bring her in the automobile to my cousin's house, and we would meet for hours. Quinton stayed tucked safely away at home with the nurse.

It was during one of these trips that Margene asked Jessie to stay with us.

"I had a dream," Margene began, "about your mama, Prissy, and my mother's maid, Kassie. They said I must trust you. And I do, Jessie. I trust you with my life."

"You won't be regretful, Miss Margene. My mama Prissy saved Mr. Alfred's life. Those doctors, they was sayin' they would use bloodlettin' to cure him. It didn't work, so they was gonna cut his leg off. My mama had a vision, and she begged Mr. Cameron to let her use the slave medicine ways to heal him. She knew if she was to fail she would die. But she loved Mr. Alfred and felt bad for him 'cause his brother got all the attention."

"What did she do?" I asked.

"She wrapped that sick foot up with roots and herbs. Kept it wrapped in bark. He had one very bad fever, sweatin' and talkin' outta his head. She stayed with him all day, all night, and after five days that fever broke and he was sittin' up and eatin' regular food. The doctor, he was some kinda mad 'cause a worthless slave had brought him back."

"Why would they care, as long as he was alive?"

"'Cause my mama, she made them shameful. She kept changing them bandages, and his foot was getting all pink-like. Then the doctor, he said enough, and he was gonna take over. And he wrapped that foot with somethin' real tight, and it turned black after a while and that doctor, he told Mr. Cameron that it was 'cause of mama that he was gonna limp his whole life."

"You mean his foot was well after your mama treated it?" Margene asked.

"Yes. I 'member 'cause at the time I was 'round two years old. And Mr. Cameron, he came to my mama and took me away and sold me to someone from the Carolinas, and said she was lucky he didn' kill her 'cause she made Mr. Alfred a cripple.

My mama, she begged and pleaded with Mr. Cameron, and she told him what that doctor had done to Mr. Alfred but no one was gonna believe a nigger slave. And that day, my mama put a curse on that family.

And then in 1863 we all got set free with the proclamation, and my momma left and started searchin' for me, and it took her ten years and she found me. And she brought me to Richmond while she was dyin', and she made Mrs. Cameron hire me on. I was 'bout 17 at the time, I guess.

And I been there ever since, to carry out mama's wishes and make sure that curse take hold of them Dunn people, for ever and always."

I knew right then and there that we had an ally for life.

October, 1908

Alfred Dunn

Father and I have been travelling for months in the South. There is much anticipation that the suffragettes will be defeated. The women are getting behind us and pushing for more and more information so that they can defeat any rabble rousers.

I have spoken to Margene several times. I must admit, I do not miss the married life, as I never had a chance to travel with Father until now. It has been wonderful, being addressed and introduced as his son. My needs are met by the two women who travel as cook and maids with us, with no fear of having to satisfy their sexual urges – only my own.

When we return to Richmond I will be running for office on the Democratic ticket that will oppose the suffrage initiative. We have a strong presence, and I believe we will be successful. I will not require Margene's participation, and will tell our constituents that she is home with our child – where she should be.

The "anti's' know that man is ordained by God to be the leader of all women. Women have a maternal role they should follow, and they should not be involved in politics. They must exercise their influence for reformation by other means, and lead through example. A woman's behavior and her service should be a gentle influence on her natural leader - the man - and she should use her gentle ways to influence him for the good. That is why my wife will not appear in public to campaign, because I want her to have her distinctive role in doing good works and helping the disadvantaged. She is first and foremost my wife and the mother of my child. She has no greater role. As much as father considers her my brood mare, I consider her my wife, and hesitate to admit I love and miss her more with each passing day.

December 1908

Margene Dunn

What a stirring meeting we had tonight with my fellow pioneers in our fight for justice. One of the women read from a letter received from abroad:

"The magnificent platform work being done from various centres must be supplemented and further spread about the world through the medium of the written word. I don't mean by frankly propagandist writing (though I am the last to deny the importance of that) but even more valuable is, I think, the spirit which both men and women writers are able in a thousand ways to illustrate and justify.

My complaint is that not enough has been made of such traces as history preserves of significant lives lived by women.

The Great Adventure is before her (woman). Your Great Adventure is to report her faithfully. So that her children's children reading her story shall be lifted up - proud and full of hope. "Of such stuff," they shall say, "our mothers were! Sweethearts and wives - yes, and other things besides: leaders, discovers, militants, fighting every form of wrong."

That night I went home and vowed to never surrender until we had the vote.

October, 1917

Margene Dunn

Alfred was elected to the Virginia State Senate last year, running on the anti-suffragette ticket as a Democrat. His father's money and connections got him elected, no doubt. He ran a family portrait in the newspapers taken some time ago showing Quinton sitting on my lap, with me seated in a chair, and Alfred standing behind me. Little did I know that portrait would be my undoing.

In September, Alfred announced he would be going on a fact-finding tour with several recently elected members of the senate. He would be accompanied by his father again. Mother Dunn did not seem to care. In a rare moment she confided, "I would gladly give him trolley fare to the local whorehouse if he would leave me alone."

We had agreed to return to the Dunn house in December, but wanted to spend the last part of fall in Deltaville. Unbeknownst to Mother Dunn, Jessie and I were headed to Washington, DC, to participate in the protests in front of the White House. Jessie, Nathan, Quinton, and I would travel to a friend's home and stay until December, then relocate to the Dunn's home in Richmond as promised. We were initially offered space in the basement office that Alice Paul has rented as our headquarters, but Nathan secured other quarters for us.

The first day on the protest stage was invigorating. We held banners that read 'Mr. President, how long must women wait for liberty?' We called ourselves the Silent Sentinels for Liberty. We protested every day except Sunday.

The United States had joined the World War I fight. After the government declared war, we were often attacked for our campaigns, as many thought we should be helping with the war effort instead. Even so, we refused to concede. Many were arrested, and all took a jail sentence instead of paying fines. The charge was 'obstructing sidewalk traffic'.

Most of the time protesters were sent to the Occoquan Workhouse. Alice Paul, one of the leaders of the movement who was sent there, was force fed by officials. Strapped down, a tube inserted – she was the bravest. These actions made some of the women abandon the movement; it only made me stronger in my resolve to see it through.

On that fateful day in early November, I took my place in front of the White House. A photographer came by and recorded the event. The next day the photograph appeared in the Washington papers, and by Friday of that week the headlines in Richmond read, *Virginia Representative Dunn Has a Suffragette Wife*. The article went on to talk about his hypocrisy in stating that I was content to be a wife and mother.

Within six days Alfred and his father returned unexpectedly from their excursion. He immediately went to Deltaville and found the house empty. Enraged, Alfred returned to Richmond, and he and his father headed for Washington, DC.

"That hussy wife of yours," Mr. Dunn screamed at Alfred. "She will ruin you. Go to Deltaville and fetch her, and bring her back here. This has to stop, Alfred. Control your wife!"

"But, father…" Alfred reportedly said.

"Alfred, Margene must be taught a lesson. She and these other willful hussies require redemption. And redemption cannot be gained without the spilling of blood."

One of the house staff, who knew of our whereabouts and was an ally of Jessie, overheard the conversation and called to warn us. Fearful for Jessie and Quinton's safety, I sent them back to Deltaville.

Alfred spent four days searching for me, and finally gave up the quest. He hired a man from Pinkerton Government Services to find me and report back. Word was, I was being hidden by Alice Paul in the basement office she had rented in Richmond. Alfred and his father returned to Richmond, determined, I am sure, to control me one way or another.

November 15, 1917

Nathan Hollister

It is so cold. I fear going to the picket lines this afternoon. The air is full of static electricity and my hair stands on end. I know Alfred and his father have plans for Margene, and I fear what those plans are. I want to believe he would not harm the mother of his child, but I cannot be certain.

All morning Margene and I go over our plan. I want to wait a week or two before we leave our secure hiding place. Margene will have nothing of it. "I will not be held prisoner by either one of those fools," she screamed at me.

"I know," I whisper, trying to comfort her. "But we have to be very careful. These are powerful, angry men, Margene. They don't care who they have to sacrifice in order to maintain their lifestyle."

Early in the morning the temperature had been in the low 30s. "It's too cold, Margene! You'll freeze walking up to the capitol mall."

"We'll wait a bit. It was warm yesterday afternoon – at least sixty degrees. No reason it shouldn't be that warm today. I have waited two days like you asked. There has been no sign of Alfred or his father."

"Margene, I just have a bad feeling about this.

"No, Nathan. I have waited long enough. We cannot hide here in the basement like trapped rats. I did as you asked."

I listened to her carefully. I knew she was not used to hiding like this. "What if they go to Deltaville and find Quinton and Jessie? They will beat her until she reveals our location. You know that they would. Then they will kill her. And what would that solve? And what of Quinton? You may never see him again."

"I don't believe that would happen. And besides," she continued, wrapping her arm around my neck. "Your 'sources' have told you that Alfred believes Quinton and Jessie are with me. I don't think they will contemplate going to Deltaville."

"Margene, please. Let's wait another day or two. I know what our spies tell us, but what if they are wrong? The risk is too great."

"I have to get out of here for a while," Margene says. "There is no discussion, Nate. I have to get out of this hole. We are going to kill each other if we don't."

Maybe she was right. We both had cabin fever and needed to get out for a short walk. No one has been around our sanctuary for days. We are far enough away that we would have noticed anyone lurking about. I finally agreed to walk up to the White House and see how the group was doing. Margene was heavily disguised. She had dusted her long hair with flour, making it appear white. We had an old pair of eyeglasses; and she removed the lenses and put them on. She had padded herself so she looked pounds heavier, and borrowed a large coat and a cane from the old woman downstairs. She looked ages older.

We started down the street. I was approximately ten paces behind her. She was bent over, shuffling along with the cane and not making eye contact with anyone on the street. I kept a safe distance, just in case someone recognized me. We believed if we travelled separately and one was caught the other had a chance to escape.

Margene turned from New York Avenue onto 15th Street. At that point, we could see the pickets in front of the White House. They were silent, except for one woman who was calling to passers-by to join their cause. Two children were running toward her, and one kicked her cane with his foot as they chased each other up the street. She fell forward, and the fall knocked her hat from her head but the rest of her disguise (thankfully) remained intact.

I noticed a man following us, but thought nothing of it. It could have been a reporter. They swarmed around the protesters these days. I expected him to help her to her feet, but he stepped back instead. He seemed to be signaling to someone ahead of us.

I started to catch up to her to help her to her feet, but saw two policemen headed in her direction, so I held back. A crowd gathered, and one of the men started to help Margene to her feet. "Let her be," the strange man behind me stated. I turned, and he announced he was with Pinkerton.

A policeman put his foot in the middle of her back, pinning her to the pavement. "She's an old woman," one of the men in the crowd shouted. "Show some respect!"

Margene struggled to stand, and a second policeman grabbed her by the arm, pinning her to the ground. "She's no old lady," he yelled to the man in the crowd. "She's one of them," he bellowed, gesturing to the protesters on the picket line. "And before the day is over, the rest of 'em will be locked up, too."

Without warning, the protesters were surrounded. Wagons pulled up and another thirty or so members of the picket line were hauled away.

"Enact the plan," were her last words to me before she was hauled off with the others.

The plan, as we had formulated it, was to go to Deltaville and get Jessie and Quinton, take the ferry to Baltimore to a safe house, and then leave for Canada. We had discussed it over and over, and now it was time to enact our battle plan.

I left that night, fearful for Margene's life, but secure in the knowledge that if there was in fact a God in heaven, we would all be safe.

I did not account for the automobile following me after I left our basement hideaway and headed for Deltaville.

Alfred Dunn

Father has ordered Margene be taken directly to the Occoquan Workhouse. The police had planned this evening's arrest to teach these silly women a lesson. They are no longer going to get away with this nonsense – refusing to eat, being let go after a day or two. No, tonight they learn their lesson. "No redemption without the shedding of blood!" Let it be if it must. I cannot go against my father. Margene has brought this upon her own head.

The conditions at the Occoquan Workhouse are well known to everyone. The blankets are washed annually at best; there are open toilets which can only be flushed from outside the cell by the guard – if the guard is willing. Women on hunger strikes are force fed.

I read of the conditions in an article by Doris Stevens in the August 11, 1917 propaganda magazine called Suffragist – a collection of pure nonsense that nevertheless should have sent waves of terror through those women

No woman there will ever forget the shock, and the hot resentment that rushed over her when she was told to undress before the entire company… We silenced our impulse to resist this indignity, which grew more poignant as each woman nakedly walked across the great vacant space to the door less shower…

This night, being naked and dealing with open toilets would be the least of the worries of these stupid cows. This night they would learn that disobedience and protest had its price.

This night, if all goes as planned, my Irish broodmare will meet with her God. Right now, however, it is my duty to follow this car which will lead me to Quinton, and I will unmask the man who has hidden her these weeks. By God, I will.

Margene Dunn

The police did not take me to court with the rest of them, not that it would have made much difference in the outcome. I still would have been sent to the workhouse. They intended to teach us a lesson, and I believe they intended to teach me in particular.

W.H. Whittaker, the superintendent of the Occoquan Workhouse, brought around forty guards into the room where we were held. They went on a rampage. Armed with clubs, they were set loose, brutalizing all thirty-three suffragists. The guards reserved their vilest rage for me. Beating me until I could not stand, they then stripped my clothing from my body, and chained my hands to the cell bars above my head. Someone threw a filthy blanket over me, and I was left there, naked and bruised, for the night. I believe they left me to die.

Later, I learned they had hurled Dora Lewis into a dark cell, smashed her head against an iron bed, and knocked her out cold. Her cellmate, Alice Cosu, believed Mrs. Lewis to be dead and suffered a heart attack. All of us, without exception, were grabbed, dragged, beaten, choked, slammed, pinched, twisted, and kicked.

I believed I was dying. I thought of my Quinton and Nathan, and the hope I once had of our lives together. I prayed that night that my death would be swift.

Quinton Dunn

My mother's cousin Herman arrived first. She had always called him Cousin Herman in front of me, just in case father ever asked. Father always thought he was a mere merchant, or sutler, as he called him. He only knew we had a man come three times a week to Deltaville to bring us food. He did not know his true identity was Nathan Hollister.

Jessie and Nathan were getting things packed up when Father arrived. He watched as Jessie loaded the car. He waited until she was back in the house, then he came storming though the door.

"Where is Mama?" I asked him, running to hug his leg.

He threw me off. "She is in prison, where she belongs, Quinton. She is probably dead by now."

"No! Mama! I want Mama!"

He turned toward Jessie. "Who is this man?" he asked between clenched teeth.

"The purveyor – Herman, the purveyor, Mr. Alfred. Please let him go. He was jus' makin' a delivery."

"Somehow, I think he is more than a purveyor, Jessie. He has been seen with Margene. I believe…"

He didn't get to finish his words because Nathan hit him full in the face with a right punch that sent him reeling. They were struggling, rolling around on the floor. I saw Father pull a pistol from behind his coat.

Jessie grabbed me, and we crashed through the door. We ran and ran, the dry fall leaves crunching under my feet. The cold air made my lungs ache, and I gasped for breath. Jessie pulled me along with her – into the woods that I hated so much.

We ran and ran, deeper and deeper. There was no moon to speak of, and it was dark. So dark and quiet, just the sound of our feet running though the leaves and the slap, slap of the river water against the bank. I hated the woods because it was where Father used to send me alone. I used to beg him not to, but he did it to punish me. Jessie and Mama would beg him, but he said I had to be a man.

We got past the first trees when I heard gunshots coming from the house. There had been loud, angry cursing and cries, then silence after the shots. We kept running, Jessie and I, until we reached the middle of the woods. It was so cold, and we huddled together and waited to see who was alive and who was dead.

"Run," Jessie said. "Run to that old root cellar and hide there. Cover yourself with the leaves. I'll keep your daddy away from you, even if he kills me. Run, Quinton, run."

And so I ran, into the dark night and the cold. I could hardly breathe; the air was so cold and dry. I didn't want to cough or make any other noises for fear Father would hear me.

I found the old root cellar and jumped in, and the leaves shielded me. They are very dry and crunchy. It has not rained in a long time, and so I sink into them. Down, down I go. It is warm, and I know no one will find me here.

Margene Dunn

The following morning a doctor arrived, I believe with the intention to pronounce me dead, and found I was still breathing. He examined my naked body and exclaimed, "Woman, you appear to be with child!"

"I am," I responded feebly. "Alfred Dunn is my husband."

"The newly elected Alfred Dunn?" he exclaimed.

"Yes," I answered and then lost consciousness. When I awoke, I was in the infirmary being attended to by a nurse.

"I have called Cameron Dunn," the doctor stated as he walked to the side of the bed. "This is most unfortunate, but you must not blame the police, for you have been seen consorting with these other women who are nihilists. He has asked that we attend to you."

I nodded.

"I also have some unfortunate news for you, but Mr. Dunn has asked that I wait until he and your mother can arrive and tend to you. I am going to give you something that will allow you to sleep."

The injection into my right thigh took mere minutes to work, and I was soon in a blissful sleep. I dreamed of Jessie and her mother covering me with blankets of fresh and fragrant herbs. I dreamed of Quinton and Nathan, playing in the sunshine. Then I dreamed of the fire.

"Margene, can you hear me?" It is my mother's voice. I am trying to wake up, running from the fire, running to Nathan.

"Margene, wake up!" It is Cameron now, talking to me through the fire. "Margene? Can you hear us?"

I drift in and out of sleep, knowing they are trying to rouse me. Nonetheless, I do not want to talk and I wait, lying very still, hoping somehow their words were part of my dream.

Quinton Dunn

It was cold outside, but now I am deep into the crispy leaves in the bottom of the cellar. I am tired, so very tired. I curl into a little ball like a mouse. It is quiet right now. No one is yelling. I wait for Jessie to come and fetch me. I am warm now – and safe. I fall asleep and suddenly Rusty is with me – just like in my nightmare. Jessie is not there, just me and Rusty.

"Rusty, Rusty – where are you? Come, boy," I yell. Rusty has been dead for many years – I know this, but I still call him to me. He runs ahead, stopping on occasion so I can follow him. My nine-year-old legs are pumping as fast as they can, and the running helps ease the cold.

Jessie comes out from behind a tree. She takes my hand and we run. There is a light in front of us. It draws us in.

A man is yelling. I cannot tell from his voice if it is Father or Nathan. I hear loud footsteps coming toward us. I am very afraid, but Jessie says to be brave. She has my hand and we are running hard toward the light. We come to the fire, a blue flame flickering and hovering above the ground.

The flame flashes and from it comes my Mama's voice. "Quinnie," she croons. "Come here and get warm with me." It is so dark that I cannot see her. Rusty is sitting before the fire, waiting for me. I walk toward my dog and the blue glow. The air smells ancient – not at all like my mother's perfumed skin.

For the first time, I am afraid. I want nothing more than to escape and go home. But someone is running toward us and I do not know if they are there to hurt me or help me. Then I see the big wooden top to the root cellar, and I jump over the side to hide in its chamber. I am quiet, not like in my dream where I am screaming for Mama. I curl up quietly in the corner of the box, hoping the person running toward me is Nathan. The walls in the box begin to grow upwards toward the sky. I try to call out, but they become higher and higher, and I realize I am a prisoner in the box.

I see Father's face glowing red and orange at the top. He is pouring something into the box, and I realize it is a lantern from the house. I smell the fuel, and the orange flame flickers above me. His face looks like a mask, all squeezed up and very angry. My father is leaning way over into the box. He is yelling down at me, "Stop being such a baby. Stop it."

My father is leaning over too far. I know this, but he is not listening, just yelling for me to shut up. Then he falls into the cellar with me, and the lantern explodes. Suddenly everything is on fire.

My back becomes very hot. I look at my arms, and the golden hairs are burning. At first I do not feel any pain, and then suddenly the blue light is all over me. I am burning, my skin is burning, and I scream but nothing comes out of my mouth. I can see the black walls now, like I am in a box with a lid and no way out

I want to stop screaming, but I cannot. I want the fire to kill me, but it does not. It is a searing that never stops. I try to suck the hot air into my lungs so I will die. I feel pain, hot and burning, and I cannot stop it. And as much as I want to, I cannot die. I keep burning and burning.

I yell to my father about the fire. He screams back, "There is no fire, Quinton."

But there is. I feel it.

Jessie appears above the box and tries to reach me. She throws a rope, and father grabs it to save himself. He pulls too hard and the rope falls on top of us. Father is screaming, trying to get out, but he cannot. Then it is quiet.

Quiet. No one is screaming. I see a woman leaning into the box and I hear Jessie call her mama. It is the black woman from my dream. She flies like a bird, swooping down into the box. She holds me to her, covers me with her green cloak. The flames retreat. My mother's voice comes from her lips. "I love you, Quinnie," she sings, over and over. It is my mother's voice coming from this black woman. She holds me to her cool body.

I feel no pain now. Just peace. I see Nathan's face above the box. "Prissy," he says. Prissy smiles up at Nathan. She holds me and we rise above the flames in the box. She takes Nathan's hand, and together we go up and up until we are far above the earth. I feel so safe and warm. I hear father's screams, but they do not scare me.

We are lifted up together toward the new light that is above us. At first it is just a pinpoint of bright, and then it grows to be the size of the sun. We go into it, the three of us.

I hear Jessie crying.

February 21, 1952

Jessie

Mr. Alfred, Quinton and Mr. Nathan all died that terrible night back there in 1917. Mr. Cameron, he had to take care of Miss Margene now 'cause she was carrying his grandchild and it was his last chance at havin' somebody to carry on the name.

'Course I knew the truth, and I told Miss Margene how Mr. Nathan tried to save Quinton, running into the woods with the bullet in him that Mr. Alfred had put in his guts. He was bleeding like crazy, but he was screaming for me and Quinton. I also knew Mr. Alfred set that boy on fire and then fell into that box with him and died a horrible death.

I saw my mama that night rising above the screaming and pain. She took Mr. Alfred and little Quinton off with her to that place we all go someday.

Mr. Nathan, he couldn't save us no how, but he sure tried. I stayed with him in the woods 'til he passed, holding him and promisin' I would take care a Miss Margene and that baby she was carrying.

Mr. Cameron had a stroke in August, 1919. He had to sit in that big old wheel chair, couldn't say nothing. We had to feed him and wash him and do everything for him. He lived another ten years, and died when he was 91. Sittin' there that whole time, big powerful man who couldn't even control his water!

Sometimes when I was visitin' with Miss Margene and her son, Nat, I would look into old man Cameron's eyes. He was fit to be tied, but couldn't say nothing. I just remember the hate.

Miss Margene, she delivered her son in May of 1918; a healthy boy he was, too. She named him Nat despite Mr. Cameron's objections. He couldn't say much as she had inherited a lotta money from Mr. Alfred and didn't need him. So he kept his mouth shut this time.

Things were changin' for women. We women got the vote in 1919. Miss Margene, she raised Nat to be a good man. He went to the College of William and Mary, and he became a fighter for people who don't have no rights. He got elected to the Virginia state senate.

I sure do wish Miss Margene coulda seen everythin' happened. She was a strong lady, but her heart done gave out back in 1930. Me, I ain't long for this world either. I'm 94 years old now, and I live with Mr. Nat and his wife Miss Victoria, in a little house next door to their big house. They take such good care a me.

In fact, Miss Victoria, she brought me here today to the senate to hear Mr. Nat get the voting rights into law in Virginia. That's right, you heard me right – it got voted in way back in 1919 but it took Virginia this long to accept it. 'Course they had to let women vote, but it weren't easy for them.

Miss Victoria is holdin' my hand as Nat Dunn gets up to speak. He got a lotta money when his grandpa died, and he turned it into scholarships for women so they could go to college. He made his mama proud.

As I watch him up on that stage, I can't help but think if he isn't the spittin' image of Nathan Hollister, then I don't know nothing!

So, I'm just waitin' to go into that light, waitin' to see everyone again. Of course, I know as well as anyone, once you go back into that light you just get on the wheel again. Round and 'round that wheel goes, sending us into the light and back out again, right back here to this world.

I'd say some peoples are gonna need to clean up some messes they made, and I gotta wonder how long it'll be before they come back again.

Me, I can't wait to see my Quinton and Mr. Nathan and Miss Margene. I just wonder when it'll be.

Bardo

Nathan

Quinton! I cannot believe my eyes. He is sitting next to me eating a huge pork chop. There are two women of color tending to him, laughing at his stories. One has a green cloak with some kind of weeds growing out of it. The other is dressed plain.

I could have sworn Quinton died in that fire in the woods. Would have sworn on my mother's grave that it happened.

But there he is, laughing and talking and eating… just as plain as day.

I wait a bit, as I want to enjoy listening to him laugh. The last couple of days there was little to laugh about. I feared I had lost Margene forever, and Quinton too. The two people I love most in the world I feared were dead and gone from me for all time.

I reach out to touch him and my hand passes through his body like he is a fog. I call out his name, but he does not respond to my voice.

"Kassie," he says to the woman in the green cloak. "This is the best pork chop! There is nothing like this in the human world. Nothing!"

The human world... where am I?

"I know it was hard for you," Kassie says as she strokes his head. "We were all so surprised when you said you wanted to go back this last time. You must truly love these people to want to help them with their process."

"I do love them. They have been with me since time began, and we all went back to try to help each other retrieve the lost pieces of ourselves that we'd left behind. I think we always leave pieces behind when we cross into that world."

"But Quinton, you are a highly evolved soul. You have been back many times and have been the one in control, the liberator, deliverer, and protector for so many. Why go back as a child who is helpless?"

"That's why I went back as the child this time. I wanted to experience the feeling of being powerless. I had never been at that level before, and my soul needed that sustenance. Just like I need this pork chop right now!"

"So, who are we waiting for?" the other woman asks.

"We are waiting for the man who was married to my mother in this last life. The man my mother loved is right here next to me. Can you see him yet?"

They were talking about me. And Alfred too, I think. And Margene. Where is my Margene?

"I think Alfred's spirit guide said Alfred was having a difficult time leaving the human life. His guide had tried to pull his spirit along, but Alfred kept going back. I don't know why – didn't his earthly body die in a fire?"

"Yes, the same fire I was in. But Kassie took my soul early, and then Nathan followed. I guess Alfred wanted to stay on a bit longer. That is using free will with disastrous results, if you ask me."

Everyone thought this quite funny.

Suddenly I realized I was not alone. I turned to my left and there sat Alfred Dunn. He was staring straight ahead as if he saw no one else in the room.

The woman Kassie, who had been tending to Quinton, came and stood in front of us. "Alfred. Welcome home," she said, touching his shoulder.

Alfred pulled back and glared at her. "I wasn't ready," he hissed through clenched teeth. "Let me go back!"

"He was dominant this time," Kassie said to no one in particular. "The ones who have human authority have the hardest time leaving."

"He is such a young soul. Nathan here – well he understood his karmic debts and how he needed to repay them. He really didn't need to stick around so long, but he wanted to. I will never understand what happens to these souls once they hit the human realm."

Quinton decided to chime in. "It's like solving a mystery. In the hundreds of times I have been back, including this last lifetime, I find humans don't learn from their experiences. They are so unaware that we souls are all connected. They don't understand it's about balancing energies – like you do something horrid to me, I do something horrid to you – we're even."

"Do they learn from that experience?" Kassie asked.

"Hopefully. The choice is theirs, after all. Sometimes it takes many lifetimes."

"I guess," Kassie said. "But aren't you angry with Alfred for setting you on fire?"

"No. Alfred was my father in the lifetime I just left. He had the power to do good, but chose to cause pain in order to maintain his control of my mother. His life was not one to imitate."

Alfred was coming out of his livid condition. He was staring straight ahead as if he were watching a baseball match. Finally he spoke. "I was horrid."

"Is he watching his life?" I asked Kassie.

"Yes. He did some good. The immature souls watch their human experience first. They need to learn it is not only the good they did, but sometimes the bad too. Because it's all a lesson. Sometimes the people that touch our lives in the human world show us how to be better souls. And sometimes they give us an example of how not to be."

"And Margene?" I asked, suddenly realizing how much I missed her.

"Ah, your true soul mate," Quinton answered. "She is a guide soul. She helped so many, including her human father, to use her to make a decision and examine our higher nature."

"Is she okay? I don't see her here."

"No, she is still back in the human realm. She is about to give birth to a child who will be quite influential in years to come. She is using the wealth provided by her marriage to Alfred for good."

"You will see Margene again, Nathan," Kassie said. "She was a true guide in your past lifetime because she allowed herself to be used by others for their own personal gain. Sometimes she showed all of you another path. Sometimes you chose right, sometimes you chose wrong. She was the channel of each of your inner desires."

"And Quinton?" I asked.

"Ah, Quinton," the other woman with Kassie said. "He was a predictor through his dreams. Because he was only a child, no one listened. Time, place, and age determined his ability to influence others. He chose that role."

Both women looked over at Quinton, who was devouring another pork chop.

"This transitioning always makes him so hungry," Kassie laughed.

"Well, we're all going back shortly...to take care of unfinished business."

"And Margene?"

"Oh, yes...she'll be here any moment. Time here isn't the same as in the human realm. In fact, I believe it is around 1930 there."

Flashes of memories of my last life were coming to me now. The beatings, Margene, her father... all of it. I closed my eyes and watched the passage of my last life and felt a longing for Margene I could not express.

And when I opened them Margene stood before me. She reached out her hand. "Let's go. We have business to tend to.

Book 4

Maggie

"We need in every community a group of angelic troublemakers."
Bayard Rustin

1963

Maggie

It was almost dying in that fire that prompted Nate to marry me. I'm not saying he wouldn't have gotten around to it eventually, but who knows what could have happened in the meantime? Everyone knows that things happen, life gets tangled up, and sometimes nothing turns out the way it's supposed to.

Sometimes I wonder if we're destined to do it over and over again until we get it right, lifetime after lifetime spent here until we've evolved enough to move on to the next world.

This makes me wonder how many people never get to move on to the next world.

My head was often full of silly thoughts like that, thoughts that popped in when I least expected it.

I leaned my head against Nate's shoulder, inhaling the scent of Old Spice and Nate, the scent that clung to his clothes. Sometimes I would take a minute in the morning, when the house was empty, and smell the empty pillowcase from our bed. I don't know how I got so lucky, but every now and then I get the feeling that our love, although imaginably predestined, was a precarious thing. Like maybe it could all go away in an instant.

Bobby Vinton's voice crooned Blue Velvet as we swayed to the music. A soft May breeze blew in through the open windows and the afternoon sunlight slanted onto the floor. I loved this song, and I loved my husband. Blue Velvet segued into Hey Paula, and we kept our arms around each other, delaying the moment Nate had to go back to the office and I had to go back to my studies.

Something crashed through the door, breaking the moment. I smiled up at Nate. "Sounds like Quinn is home."

Kissing me on top of my head, he held me close for a moment. "The kid always did have good timing."

"Oh, gross!" Quinn's young voice rang out as he passed through the living room on his way to the kitchen. "Mom, what's for lunch?"

"Did you wipe your feet before coming in here?" I asked. "Go wash your hands and I'll make you something."

Nate was moving toward the couch, shaking his head while he gathered his briefcase and suit jacket. "We should make a record of you saying that to him, you know."

I laughed. "While you're at it, we can make a record of it for you, too."

"No doubt about it, he's my son," Nate said. "I'll be home a little bit late tonight, but not too late. I've got a meeting that shouldn't take long."

I shivered. I knew what that meant. "Who did you find this time?"

My husband, the love of my life, tried to play innocent. "Find?"

"Who are you interviewing?" I asked. Nate was not like me at all. I believed that everything happened for a reason, and people should let go of things that serve them no good in this life. But Nate is a lawyer with a strong sense of fairness and justice, and cannot stand to see any bad deed go unpunished. Especially a bad deed that almost killed his wife.

"His name is Joshua," Nate admitted. "He is the little boy that lived in the house down the street when the fire broke out. Of course it's been eleven years, so he's older now. I don't expect he'll remember much, but any little thing might help."

"When are you going to let this go? Nobody died, and it happened over a decade ago. What do you plan to do after all this time?" I did not understand Nate's drive to uncover the truth of what happened, since it was so long ago and everybody was fine. If I was honest about it, I'd have to say I was more than a little scared of what he would do if he ever did find out who set the fire.

That period in my life was an incredible mixture of love and fear, and I believe it altered my future in so many ways.

In 1951 I was living with my Aunt Victoria in her home on Richmond Road in Williamsburg, Virginia. My parents had agreed to let me go to college with the stipulation that I live with a relative off-campus. They lived in Danville, and were concerned about me being so far from home and all alone. It was decided that going to college in Williamsburg was ideal, since Aunt

Victoria had plenty of room in her rambling old house. It was also perfect because my aunt and I got along so well, and I adored her and her slightly eccentric ways.

Aunt Victoria was a collector of oddities, strange things brought from far and distant lands. She had African masks, Celtic crosses, Tibetan statues and Indian pottery. Her books covered a range of topics, from Buddhism to witches. She loved debating theology, and often challenged me to think of the Universe in a broader sense, as more than just what we could see or touch at any given time.

My aunt was widowed, and she believed strongly in the magic of love. She told me so as soon as I started dating Nathaniel.

I met Nate in our philosophy class, where we argued over what Heidegger meant by 'the authentic self'. As soon as class ended, he asked me out to dinner so we could continue the argument. I was terrified of being pulled into a relationship like the other girls I'd seen in my college classes. Once they started dating someone, they left school and got married, something I vowed would not happen to me. I put him off for a week because I didn't know what to say, but in the end relented.

Nate and I had the best time on our dates, laughing and talking and getting to know each other. We were attending the College of William & Mary, and although we were crazy in love and spending every waking moment together there was one thing that was a dark spot in our world. It was his mother, Alice Kay. Alice Kay was doing everything in her power to keep her baby boy away from me. She didn't think I was good enough for her son, and naturally she had someone else in mind for him. Someone with good breeding, who came from a prominent Virginia family. A proper wife, one who would present her with an heir to carry on whatever legacy she'd created in her own mind.

I'm not angry with Alice Kay, because I understand that she is who she is. I don't blame her, but I know that she has never done anything that did not further her own agenda. She can't help it, and I have to wonder how Nate turned out to be such a kind person after being raised by that type of mother.

Of course we were having sex back then, before we were married, which I'm certain his mother was well aware of. I don't think she knew because Nate told her, I think she knew because she already assumed I was a tramp. At the time I figured I might as well go

the entire cottage for myself. It was small, but because of the graciousness of my aunt, it was my space. It was perfect.

It was May, and I remember it was a warm, flawless spring day. I'd been hard at work in the little house when I heard a tentative knock at the door.

"Come in," I called. When Aunt Victoria opened the door, I looked up from my work and smiled. "Auntie Vic, you don't have to knock. This is your house, after all."

"I know you tell me that dear, but I don't want to disturb your studies. This is important work you're doing, and I would rather not be in the way."

"You're never in the way," I protested. Pushing my safety goggles to the top of my head, I noticed she was wearing her long, tailored suit jacket with matching skirt, and pulling on gloves. Aunt Vic was not usually one to wear skirts, as most of the time she was puttering around in the garden. "Are you going out?"

A sigh accompanied her remark. "Yes. I received an exceptionally late-notice invitation yesterday to attend a dinner party."

"It will be good for you to go," I told her. In my opinion, my aunt needed to socialize more and spend some time having fun. She was a focused woman with many causes, but I believed that a balanced life was important for good health. "Haven't I told you that you'll feel better in the long run if you go out and enjoy yourself? I can make all the potions in the world, but they won't help you if you're not working on maintaining balance in your life. Work and fun."

"I know dear, but there's something a bit odd about this invitation. It came from an old friend whom I have not seen in years, and she was a bit insistent that I attend her dinner tonight. Downright pushy, actually, which is rather unusual of her."

"She must not be from the South," I said, lowering my head to hide the smirk. It was a joke between my aunt and I that Southern girls were the most polite, well-behaved, proper girls in the country. They weren't, really, they just played the part so well that most of them believed their own propaganda.

I could see that my aunt was hiding a grin of her own. "Now Maggie, try to remember your manners."

"Yes, ma'am. Anyway, you have fun tonight."

"Thank you, dear. And, Maggie, one more thing… try not to get too engrossed in your studies. I know that this is fascinating, and I believe important, work that you're doing, but you must remember to have a little fun of your own. Isn't that young man of yours taking you anywhere tonight?"

I smiled. I loved that my aunt understood me and my passion for healing so well. "No, it's just me and the books tonight. Nate has to study, so he's getting together with a group of the other students to get ready for his exam."

"Don't stay out here too late, then. The back lights haven't been working and I don't want you stumbling around in the dark. I should be home early, as I expect I'll have a headache coming on tonight. Goodnight, dear."

"Goodnight, auntie," I said, smiling at her comment about getting a headache. My aunt's headaches were a remarkable convenience.

Once she left, I turned my attention back to my book. I was having trouble concentrating, but tried to stay focused. The thing I remember most is reading and re-reading the passage about linseed oil. According to my book, the oil is made from flax and has been used for centuries. Unfortunately for me, I had a very good memory of what it tasted like, as my mother used to force it on me for various ailments when I was a child.

The memory of that taste caused my stomach to roll. I grasped the antique necklace I wore, given to me years ago by Aunt Victoria. When she gave it to me she told me it had both protective and healing qualities and that it had saved a life or two. I held the amulet, hoping it might impart some type of healing to help me through this strange stomach affliction. This time, however, it had no affect on me. If anything, I felt worse.

Not wanting to be sick in the little house, I dashed outside and ran into the main house. I barely made it to the bathroom before retching. It was over in a minute, and I cleaned myself up, determined to get some work done that night. Stomach virus. I should be fine by tomorrow.

Walking to the back door, I thought about what I would create that evening. I didn't want to wander too far from the house, so gathering herbs was probably not a good idea.

As I started to push the door open, I stopped, suddenly terrified.

My little house in the back yard was engulfed in flames.

Quinn

I don't want to be scared of anything. I want to be brave, like Amos Burke in the television show *Burke's Law*. Amos is a police detective, and he's rich and handsome and smart, and of course he always catches the bad guy at the end. He's never afraid of things, especially things that haven't even happened yet.

I want to be like him, especially since he is driven around in a Rolls Royce Silver Cloud. That car was far out, and it's gotta be great to have a chauffeur. Mom says the important thing in life is to be kind to people and happy with what you've got. I know she's right, but sometimes I think it's probably easier to do if you are someone like Amos Burke.

Burke's Law was on Friday nights at 8:30, and I never missed an episode. It came on right after *77 Sunset Strip*, which was alright, but sometimes it could be a little silly. We didn't watch much television at our house, but I was allowed to watch it on Friday nights. Usually I stayed up late at night, anyway, reading in bed until my mom yelled at me to go to sleep.

The thing about being eleven years old is that nobody really notices you. I don't mean my mom and dad, although sometimes that happens when they're busy, but people in general. It's like I'm not really in the room sometimes, and adults will talk as if they had nothing to hide.

And I figured out pretty quickly that there are some adults that have plenty to hide.

My parents are good people, but sometimes I think they don't really understand that there are others who are not so good. My dad gets it, I mean, he is a lawyer, and he sees all kinds of criminals and stuff. But my mom, she has this idea that people are essentially good and that there's more to this world than we understand.

She might be right about the world, but from what I've seen there's lots of bad in lots of people. But I'm just a kid, so I keep my mouth shut.

The thing is, my mom is really anxious for change. She thinks that there's a whole new movement happening right now, and our country is on the verge of something big. She has trouble seeing that the 'something big' might be 'something bad'.

I've been watching my parents and their friends, and all I can say is I'm ready. I've heard the things that have been said, and some of those people give me the creeps. I wonder if my parents know what some of their friends are up to.

I have a weird feeling that my mom is going to need protection; I know that's why she wears the thing around her neck. People always think that a little bit of magic can make anything better. But just in case it isn't magic, I'll be there.

My dad has a friend, Al. They've been friends forever. Anyway, these people that Al is hanging out with, I've been listening to them, and they don't know I'm listening. I blend right in.

My mom is right about one thing, change is definitely coming. I think the change is going to hurt her, though.

I'm not going to let anyone hurt her, no matter what.

Nate

There's something very satisfying in hearing the solid thunk when my fist makes contact with the bag. Over and over, the rhythm of hitting is what heals me.

I do believe in the therapeutic value of boxing, despite my wife's declaration of wanting to live a non-violent lifestyle.

"Nate, we have to work on finding that place of peace within ourselves and expressing that to the world," she told me.

"That's why I box," I said.

"But it's a violent sport, Nate. Perhaps there's another way you can release your tension?"

I teased her a little then, detailing a few different ways I could release tension. She just laughed and swatted at me, pretending to be horrified by the suggestion.

"Fine, go hit your bag if you must," she said. "I guess everyone has a different way of being in this world, and if it helps you to release your anger then go ahead. As long as you don't hurt anyone, I suppose it's fine."

My intention has never been to hurt another person, with one exception. I want to find whoever set fire to Maggie's studio and destroy them.

I don't think I have it in me to actually kill someone, but the fact is that I believe someone tried to murder my wife, the woman I love. I don't know why anyone would do that, but I know that fire was no accident. I never told Maggie about the conversation I had with the police chief, as I didn't see where it would do any good for her to know.

Mitchell Sommers was a great hulking man, and he loved his work. He'd gotten a job with the police department as soon as he was old enough to work, and had become the youngest police chief ever. His appointment to the position happened right around the time of Maggie's fire.

"What was in there, Nate?" he asked.

"Books and things Maggie was studying," I said. I remember clasping my hands behind my back, trying not to show how badly the incident had shaken me.

Mitchell leveled a stern look at me. "If you want to tell me the truth, I'm here to listen."

"What are you saying? Why would I lie about what was in there?" I'd known Mitchell my entire life, and at that time he was dating my sister, Kathy. I didn't want to believe he was insinuating there was something more going on at that time.

"Listen, I know you don't want to hear this, but someone wanted that building to burn, and they wanted it to burn good," he told me. "There's evidence that the fire was deliberately set. Now, I'll ask you again, did Maggie or that aunt of hers have anything to hide?"

I was younger then, and a little bit more foolish than I am today. I told Mitchell exactly what he could do with his idea that Maggie or anyone in her family had something to hide, then I stalked around the corner, found her on the side of her aunt's house, and asked her to marry me. Just like that.

I never wanted to lose her, and that fire made me realize that there are some things in this world you should not take for granted. Love was at the top of that list.

Thankfully Maggie said yes, so we got married pretty quickly. Good thing, too, because eight months later Quinn was born. That's right, eight months, but who's counting? Actually, I think my mother might have been, but I cannot live my life for her or her strange ideas of societal conventions.

Mitchell's words stayed with me over the years, and I know now, just as I knew on that day, that someone tried to kill Maggie. It's possible I didn't want to know who did it or why, but the fact was that I couldn't let it go.

I mean, someone tried to kill her. Anyone who knew about that little house knew that Maggie was in it all the time, studying her botany textbooks and creating salves and teas and all sorts of remedies. The whole situation still makes me uncomfortable.

Maggie wants to know what difference finding the arsonist makes, and cannot understand why I won't let this go. I don't want to tell her that I'm terrified, both for her and Quinn. What if it's not over? What if the person who tried to kill her comes back to finish the job?

Maybe I was so worried because we lived in that same house now. Maggie had inherited the house from Aunt Victoria when she died at the ripe old age of 87, and I knew Aunt Victoria wanted Maggie, Quinn and me to be as happy in the house as she had been. She'd talked about it in the weeks prior to her death, and I know it pleased Aunt Victoria in the end that she'd been able to provide something substantial to her favorite, and only, niece.

But the fact remains; I am haunted by that fire. I can still see the flames in my dreams at night, feel the heat as if it was burning me, and I try to reach Maggie and run for it. The problem is, it's a dream, so in that realm it's not just Maggie threatened by the fire, it's Quinn, too. My wife and son are in danger, and even though it's an imagined, dreamtime danger, that terrifies me more than anything.

The problem is that I have no idea why anyone would want to hurt Maggie, so I have no way of protecting her from this unknown darkness.

So, I'm doing the only thing I can for now. I'm investigating every last piece of information I can find, interviewing people who may have seen something or know something.

I will not let my family get hurt. I will die protecting them if I have to.

Maggie

"Well, hello pretty lady," the voice murmured behind me.

I bit back the sigh of exasperation that almost escaped. I know Al meant well, and he thought he was just being silly, but frankly I didn't like it when he snuck up on me. Especially in my own house.

"Al, how are you? What brings you all the way out here tonight?" I really needed to remember to lock the back door, but I hated the thought of a house locked up tight. I wanted to live in a house full of life and warmth, not a prison. But I didn't like it when Al came right in without announcing himself.

"I thought if I got here early maybe you'd change your mind and decide you loved me after all," he said, waggling his eyebrows at me. Straightening to his full height of almost six feet, he stroked his mustache in what I'm certain he thought was a beguiling manner. "Perhaps you and I could…"

"I'm a married woman, Mr. Portwell. I would not betray my husband in that way."

"Same thing you said in college, Maggie. It was always going to be a 'no' for me, wasn't it?"

"Gee, Al, you sure know how to make a girl feel welcome in her own home," I said. What was he thinking, saying things like that?

Al had the grace to at least try to look abashed, but I knew this was some kind of weird game for him. Did he really think that I would have an affair with my husband's best friend? I knew Al from years ago, when my uncle used to work in his family's steel business. The Portwell family was entrenched in area politics, and had been for centuries as far as I knew. They had money and ambition, the two things necessary to be successful in that field.

I couldn't stand the sight of Al, but I tried to hide that small fact. I told Nate many times about the little suggestions Al made about the two of us getting together, trying to disguise them as jokes. I never wanted that sort of thing to come between Nate and me, and I never hid anything from him.

Unfortunately for me, Nate didn't take these things too seriously. "He's just kidding around with you. He doesn't really mean it." That's what my husband truly believed, so I didn't cause too much of a scene when Al said the things he said. I think the real reason my husband didn't believe it was because it never entered his mind that his old friend could be so devious. My husband may have been an attorney, but he mostly practiced estate law, writing wills and handling probate matters. He sometimes witnessed vile human behavior related to arguments over bequests, but in general Nate believed in the innate goodness of mankind.

This was why I didn't let Al get away with it. My husband may have a streak of naiveté, but that would not mean I had to let his friend get away with being a jerk.

Al was wandering through the hallway, headed toward the living room at the front of the house. This time I didn't stop the sigh, since I knew I'd have to follow him.

"Don't you get nervous, being in this big house all by yourself?" he asked. "Or maybe lonely?"

This was new. Usually when Al said something suggestive to me he let it go as soon as I told him no. It wasn't like him to be persistent.

"No, I'm fine. Nate should be home later if you wanted to see him."

Al stopped and looked at me with a direct gaze that made me want to hide in a closet somewhere. "What about Quinn? When does that boy of yours get home?"

"Why? What's this all about? You're acting funny, Al. What's going on?"

"I just came from your sister-in-law's house," he said. "Her and that police chief husband of hers, nice people. I know I've got their support, they made that clear."

It took me a moment to understand what Al was talking about. "Support of what?" I felt like an idiot for asking, and I'm sure he knew that. Al liked to make people feel small.

Al's smile sent a chill through me. "I'm running for office, Maggie girl. And not town council, either. I'm going big time, now. You're looking at the next United States Senator."

Quinn

I do not like Mr. Portwell. He's one of those people who never notices kids, so he's never really seen me when I've been around him. Sure, once in a while he acknowledges I'm there, but for the most part he acts like I don't even exist.

He's not a nice person. I've watched him do things when he didn't know anyone was looking. He pinches women on the butt, he takes things that don't belong to him, and he's mean to small animals. And, I've heard him lie to people, say one thing to one person and the exact opposite to someone else.

I do not understand why my father is friends with him. I asked Mom about it once, and she said that Dad believed that deep down inside people were truly good. She also said it was hard for Dad to see anything negative about people he cared about. I told Mom she should tell Dad everything Mr. Portwell says, because Dad needs to know. She just shrugs and says she can handle it.

I know Mom doesn't like Mr. Portwell, either, because he's always flirting with her and trying to get her to kiss him. It's gross, but my mom handles it pretty well. I don't know why she doesn't just slap him, but I guess my mom has more class than that.

I was in the other room when Mr. Portwell came over today, and I heard him tell Mom about his plans to become a Senator. Great, just what our country needs, another lying politician to maintain the status quo. That's a term I learned in English class this year, and I love using it. People always look surprised when they hear kids say things like 'status quo'.

Mr. Portwell doesn't know that I've seen him with his other friends, out at the old farmhouse. I ride my bike all over the place, and I stumbled on one of their meetings. It scared me, but I forced myself to stay hidden and watch what they were doing. It's what Amos Burke would have done.

I didn't tell anyone, because I'm not sure who to tell. I don't know who else is part of that group, and I don't want to put myself or my family in danger.

My parents and I talk about politics a lot, and we talk about where this country is heading. We talk about our president, John F. Kennedy, and nuclear war and the Cuban missile crisis. We talk about civil rights and the change Martin Luther King, Jr. is working so hard to make happen, and we talk about what it will be like when that change happens.

If that change happens. If it doesn't, it will be because of those people I saw at that old farmhouse, Mr. Portwell and his friends.

I know what they're doing in there, too.

Maggie

Al wouldn't leave. I tried to drop subtle hints, but he insisted on waiting for Nate to get home. I didn't know what to do, so I sat in the living room with him, sipping iced tea and waiting for my husband.

I'm sure Al knew I was nervous. I kept rubbing at my wrists, a habit I've had since childhood. I have birthmarks around both wrists, strange shapes that almost look as if I'm wearing a bracelet on each arm.

Or maybe shackles, depending your perspective.

Then I started twisting my necklace, the same one I'd been wearing the night of the fire, the necklace my aunt said would protect me. Al gave me a funny look, started to say something, then stopped.

Finally Nate walked through the door, and I could tell he was tired. I knew the interview hadn't gone well, but I didn't want to discuss it right then. Al always had this weird smirk on his face when the subject of the fire came up, and he'd tease me about it, saying things like "You must've forgotten to put your cigarette out, Miss Maggie." I have never smoked, can't stand inhaling that stuff into my lungs. It seems pretty clear to me that it's bad for you, but nobody believes me.

"Hello, my friend, what brings you here?" my husband asked, shaking Al's hand.

"Good news, Nate, good news," Al said, standing.

"Let me get you something to drink," I said, and left the room. I hoped that whatever Al had to say about running for office, he would say it and leave. I certainly wasn't going to vote for him, but I knew my husband would want to talk politics with Al.

From the kitchen, I could hear the murmur of voices. Quinn sat at the table, stirring his milk and Ovaltine.

"Mom, can I tell you something?"

"Does it have to do with Mr. Portwell?"

My beautiful son looked so unhappy. "I think he's gonna do something bad," he said.

I didn't know what to say, because I agreed with Quinn. There was a feeling around Al tonight, a feeling of recklessness and danger. It wasn't anything I could put into words, but I sensed a darkness around Al. I believe every mother faces this kind of predicament at some point. We know there is darkness, but how much should we tell our children? How could I protect Quinn from all the evils in the world, while at the same time prepare him for the bad things that inevitably happen around us?

"You may be right," I said. "But all we can do is stand on the side of goodness and light."

"I don't see how that will stop Mr. Portwell," Quinn pouted.

"It might not," I answered. "But we cannot always stop bad things from happening. All we can do is set an example for other people, show them what it means to live from a place of love, forgiveness and healing."

"You're the only mom I know who says things like that," Quinn said.

I smiled. "I know. But times are changing, and I think you'll hear more and more of this kind of thinking. Look at the Rev. Martin Luther King, Jr. He always talks about love and forgiveness overcoming hate."

Quinn walked back into the living room with me, helping me carry drinks to the men.

"But there's still lots of people who don't like him, not because of what he preaches, but because of the color of his skin," Quinn said.

"I know, but you can't deny that he's right," I answered.

"Who doesn't like someone?" Al asked.

"We were talking about the Rev. Martin Luther King, Jr.," I said.

Al's face contorted. "We do not need to be discussing that type of rabble-rousing trash. In fact, let's talk about my invitation to you, since we're on the subject."

"What are you talking about?" I asked. But I knew before he even said it, I knew in my heart what Alfred was going to offer us. I think I've always known, deep down inside, about Alfred Portwell and what kind of person he really is.

Nate

My heart hurt when my old friend Al opened his mouth and started talking.

Where does all this hate come from? Why do people insist on living like this? It hurt to hear him say those things, but it made me angry, too.

I don't pretend to understand human nature, I leave that to my wife. But I do understand decency and goodness, and what Al was talking about had nothing to do with anything decent or good.

"Al, we've known each other for years. You know me better than that," I said.

My old childhood friend looked at my wife sideways before answering. "This may be a little much for the wife and kid, Nate," he said. "Why don't you send them away?"

I clenched my jaw, hoping to regain some measure of control. It would not look good to deck a man who had not even threatened me, despite the many ways I felt threatened and violated.

Al and I had known each other since we were kids. Our parents were friends, and our mothers were debutantes the same year. We endured cotillion together, hating the dances and the gatherings we were forced to attend, but together we learned all the niceties of formal society.

And now my old friend, the one I thought I knew so well, is standing in front of me telling me he's joined an organization dedicated to the elimination of the negro.

"Don't get me wrong, Nate, we're not the KKK," Al said. "Those men, they're out of control. They do good work, but they lack a certain finesse, don't you think?"

All I could do was stare. Until that very moment, I had no idea my friend was so full of poison. Obviously, Maggie was right. I was completely naïve.

"Our goal is more political. Those KKK guys, they go around killing folks and stirring people up, which is fine, but we're getting to the heart of the problem. Byrd gave us a start with massive resistance, keeping all those blackies out of our schools, but we've got so much more work to do. That's why I'm running for Senate, to carry on the work."

United States Senator Harry F. Byrd had been a huge proponent of segregation, and worked diligently to uphold what was known as the 'Southern Manifesto', an ideology that supported racism. The Byrd machine was vile, creating laws that cut off state funding and closed schools that decided to desegregate.

I did not speak a word, not one word. Al interpreted my silence as acquiescence.

"So, I know that I have your support, but I wanted to personally invite you to our next meeting. We're not like those others, we don't have robes or meet in secret, but I think you'll be surprised at the amount of power that gathers in one room. We are a formidable group of men who have firm political standing, that's the truth. God is on our side, Nate."

"There is no God that would condone such hateful, nasty behavior." My wife's voice rang through the room.

Al sat down and proceeded to light a cigar. "This is why you have to get the womenfolk out of the way, Nate. They never understand philosophical or political conversations."

My fists clenched. "Do not speak of my wife in that manner. She is smarter than most men I know."

Al leaned forward and took a drink from Maggie's hand, tossing it back. "Nate, you need to relax a little. You're wound up too tight these days. So, what do you say? Will you join us in our cause? I know your mother would love to see you do the right thing, for once."

"My mother would not be happy about this," I said.

I could see Maggie hesitate, wanting to say something but changing her mind. Al simply smiled.

"She wouldn't, my mother would never condone this type of behavior," I insisted. "She's…" I stopped, unsure of what to say. She was my mother, and although she never showed us lots of affection when we were children I refused to believe she would take part in such a heinous activity. I would like to think that I got my moral bearings in this world because of the way I was raised, and if my mother were a racist, evil-hearted woman I would have known by now. Surely I would have seen some sign of that.

"There's more to your dear mother than you realize," Al said. "So, can I count on you? Maybe you don't want to attend my meetings yet. I can see you have some work to do with the little woman on that one. But surely I've got your vote this fall, right?"

I shook my head. "Al, we've known each other our whole lives. But this thing… this goes beyond our friendship. I cannot, and I will not, condone hatred." In truth, I wanted to punch him. I had never pictured a day when I would have to say these words to a friend. "I'm sorry, but I will not vote for you. I'm not even sure I can be your friend right now."

Silence sat in the room, accompanied only by the ticking of the clock. I could see my son's wide eyes, watching me, and in that moment I was glad of what I had said. Friend or not, I needed to set an example for Quinn, and teach him about treating people well, regardless of the color of their skin.

I took a deep breath. "I'm going to have to ask you to leave now, Al."

Al held up a hand. "Wait a minute, just one minute. You can't tell me you don't feel the same way I do. Why, think about it. Those people, if you can call them that, they are ruining our chances for a civilized society here in Virginia. Some of the recent changes that those Yankees are trying to bring about relative to the darkies are a clear threat to our gentlemen's way of life. You can't just sit back and let that happen."

I did not need to hear any more of this. This person I had once called friend was a stranger after all. All those years I'd put up with him and his supercilious ways, all those years I'd listened to him brag about things he should not have spoken of in polite company, all those years of spending time with a man who was nothing more than a rotten, cheating schemer.

"I'm sorry you feel that way. I'm sorry I've wasted time on a friendship that resulted in this. Get out of my house, and don't come back," I said.

Al looked at me and laughed. "I do believe you need to get your priorities straight, Nathaniel. You should think twice before throwing me out of your house. Why, what would your family say to this type of behavior?"

"Not only do I want you out of my house, I am going to work as hard as I can to fight your political aspirations, whether it's the Senate or the town council. I will expose you for who you really are, and I will expose that so-called secret society of yours. The people have a right to know they're being manipulated."

Al stood, his face grim. "Be careful trying to threaten me, old friend. I would hate to see something happen to this beautiful family of yours. You might want to think twice before 'exposing' me."

Without another word, he turned and walked out my front door.

Maggie

I did not want my son to see how scared I was. Tonight, in my own home, a man just walked right in and frightened me witless. Grasping the old amulet I wore that my aunt had given me long ago, I prayed it truly did hold the magic it was rumored to possess. We could use a little of that right now. Shoving aside my fear, I put on a brave front. "Isn't it time for you to start getting ready for bed?" I said, turning to Quinn and stroking his face.

He hugged me, hard. "It's going to be okay, mom, don't worry."

"I know, son, I know." But I was worried. It was clear from what happened tonight that Al was a man on a mission, a man who was connected to powerful people and set on committing horrific acts.

Discomfort rode through me in waves, making me nauseous. What if Al wanted to hurt us? What if he decided to hurt my son to stop Nate from exposing his secrets? I would not lose my family to such a depraved group of people, that secret society Al spoke of.

"Go on upstairs, I'll be up in a little while," I said to Quinn. I know my boy didn't want to go upstairs, but he did it anyway.

When I knew he was out of earshot, I turned to my husband and crossed my arms over my chest. Nate and I stared at each other for a moment, too stunned to speak.

"What was that?" he whispered. "Was he always like that?"

My eyes filled with tears as I nodded my head. I knew it hurt my husband to hear this, and I knew he felt betrayed, but I would not lie to him.

"Remember all those times I told you about him flirting with me, and how it made me uncomfortable? He is not a nice man, and even your son has noticed that. Quinn said something to me earlier about Al, about how he didn't like him." I stopped talking for a moment, steeling myself to ask the question that needed to be asked.

"Nate, what do you think he's going to do?"

Nate gave a short, brittle laugh. "How can I know what he's going to do when I didn't even realize what he was already doing?" Covering his face with his hands, my husband sank onto the couch. "Maggie, who the hell have I been friends with all these years?"

I sat beside Nate, lightly rubbing his back. I have often said that betrayal from your friends is the worst kind of betrayal. I don't mean to diminish the pain of spousal or familial betrayal, but our friends know us best, they know our secrets and our desires. They know who we are and they know where we've been. Our friends are supposed to be the ones that help us pick up the pieces, not the ones that create the mess.

"We need to make certain he does not come back and hurt either you or Quinn," Nate said, sitting up straight.

"We're certainly not going to let him back in this house," I said. "So I don't see how he could hurt us."

"You're not in the house all the time," Nate said. "And it's clear that he's not who I thought he was. How do we know what he's capable of? What if he's done things to other people, and we never knew about it? I know his family, and I know he's got the money and power to do whatever he wants. We need to take steps to protect you."

"Nate, let's think this through. You're right; I'm not in the house all the time. But by the same token, I think we need to take care of Quinn first. If you consider the fact that he's constantly outside, riding his bike all over town, then logically that puts him in the most danger."

Nate stood and began to pace. "When does Quinn finish the school year?"

"He doesn't have much time left. They get out in June, but he's so ahead in his class work that it won't matter if we pull him out now. He'll still move on to sixth grade next year."

"Let's do that, then. Will you go with him to visit your parents?" Nate asked.

I hesitated. It was a great idea for my son to visit his grandparents, but I was not so sure I wanted to be in Danville, Virginia. "I think Quinn and my parents would have a great time together, and I know they'd love to have him," I began.

"They'd love to have you, too," he said.

"That's true, but I really feel like it's important to be here with you."

Nate blew out a frustrated sigh. "Maggie, you heard what Al said. He basically warned us, telling us he was going to do something terrible to you and Quinn. I cannot have you here in this town."

I stood to my full height of five feet five inches when I answered him. "And I will not be run out of my own home by some low-down, scheming piece of worm anus that thinks he can waltz in here and turn my life upside down." I took a breath, trying to calm my racing heart. "I agree, we should protect our son, but I will not run like a coward. I'm staying here, with you."

I couldn't read Nate's expression, and that made me nervous. Normally I knew exactly what my husband was thinking.

"I won't tell you what to do," he said. "I don't like it, but I understand. The only thing I ask is that we stay in constant contact. Don't go anywhere alone without me knowing, and I'll make sure you always know where I am."

"No more late night meetings," I said.

Nate shook his head. "As much as I hate to say it, you're right. For now, no more late night meetings."

"I'll call my parents and make the arrangements," I said. As I walked toward the phone, a thought struck me. I spun around, facing my husband. "Nate, he said something before you came."

"Did he hurt you?"

I shook my head. "No, but he was talking about Mitchell and your sister. He said he had their support. What do you think that means?"

Nate's brow furrowed as he considered my words. "That's pretty serious if Al has the backing of the chief of police."

"I know," I said. "And it would mean that they support his… ideas."

"I'll check in with my sister later," Nate said. "For now, go call your mother. I don't want Quinn staying here another night if it's not safe."

I agreed. I would not let Alfred Portwell hurt my child.

Quinn

I didn't mind that I had to go spend time at my grandparents' house, because I really liked being with them. They're pretty cool, and I always have lots of fun hanging out with my grandfather. He's an easygoing person, and he's always got something interesting to talk about. Plus, he takes me fishing. I don't especially like fishing, but I like spending long, lazy days on the Dan River. We might not always come home with supper, but we sure have lots of fun trying.

The only thing that bothered me was leaving my mom alone in the house. I knew my father would take care of her, but he had to go to work and sometimes she'd be left alone. But she said she refused to be pushed out of her own house, and that if a battle was going to be fought she would stand right next to her husband and fight. If I was there, I could protect her and make sure that weenie Al didn't hurt her.

Summer in Virginia is hot, and it was especially warm when I got to Gram and Gramps house. It was the end of May, but those of us in the South considered that to be summer, no matter what the calendar said.

I'd spent a lot of time in Danville over the years, and had a few friends in town. I was excited to see some of my friends and let them know I'd be hanging out for the summer.

I rode to Danville the same way my mother and I had always ridden there, on the train. My mother dressed in a long, man's coat and took me to the train station after driving all over town first. I think if anyone had followed us, they would've been confused. We got to the train station and I had to sit in the front car, so the people who worked there could keep an eye on me. The conductor reassured me mother repeatedly that kids traveled alone all the time on the train, and I would be fine.

Of course, he didn't know about Al, and my mother never mentioned it.

When we got to Danville, I scrambled to pull my suitcase out of the overhead compartment. As soon as I got off the train, I saw my grandparents waiting for me. My grandma hugged me so hard it hurt.

"Ow," I said. "Why are you squeezing me so hard?"

She had tears in her eyes when she answered. "Because I've missed you."

"Because my mother told you I'm in danger," I said. "But I'm fine, really. That big weenie didn't get anywhere near me."

Grandpa kind of coughed, and I knew he was trying not to laugh. He put an arm around me, grabbed my bag and started leading me out to the car. "C'mon, son. We've let folks know you're coming, some of your friends are anxious to see you."

"Oh my goodness, that Eddie Williams has been by the house four times already, wondering if you'd gotten here yet. I told him I would send you over to see him as soon as you got in."

Eddie is my best friend in Danville. He and I have known each other forever, and have always hung out when I'm in town. One summer he got permission to spend a couple of weeks in Williamsburg, which was really fun. I showed him around and we had the best time. His parents are friends with my parents, and he has an older sister who pretty much stays out of our way. Sometimes people who see us together mistake us for brothers, since we both have the same brown hair and freckles.

Once we got to my grandparent's house on Pine Street, I ran inside and up the stairs to my room. It was an older house, and my room was the guest room on the second floor. I always slept there when I visited, and I still had my toy cars and Lincoln Logs in the closet.

I threw my bag on the bed and ran back downstairs. "I'm going over Eddie's house," I called out.

"Don't you want something to eat?" my grandmother asked.

"No, I'll eat later." I knew that Eddie's mother would load us up with apples and sandwiches before we went anywhere, and I didn't want to wait much longer. I had to talk to Eddie, tell him what happened.

"I took your bike out of the shed and put it on the side of the house," my grandfather said. "Be back by six o'clock, your grandmother will have our meal ready by then."

I pedaled as hard as I could and got to Eddie's house on Paxton Avenue in under two minutes. He didn't live far, but we always tried to find ways to get to each other's houses faster.

He was sitting on the front steps to his porch, and as soon as he saw me he jumped up and hopped on his bike. "Quinn's here, Mom," he yelled at the front screen door. "We're going to ride our bikes." Lifting a paper bag at me, he nodded. I knew he had food, so we were prepared.

I didn't have to ask him where we were going, because I knew we would head over to our spot by the river. Sure enough, I followed Eddie through the streets, not far to a secluded location. We hopped off our bikes and put them down and walked a little ways to the edge of the Dan River.

"I heard you got yourself into some trouble up in Williamsburg," Eddie said.

I shrugged. "It's not really trouble, but that weenie Al threatened me. My parents think I'm in some kind of danger, so they sent me here to keep me safe."

"I guess they don't know, then," Eddie said.

"Don't know what?"

"That you might be in danger here, too. Haven't you heard? It's all anyone around here is talking about. There's something called the Freedom Movement happening in Danville, and people are practically fighting in the streets."

"What are you talking about?" I asked.

"I'm talking about the whole civil rights thing," Eddie said. "People here are mad, really mad. I guarantee, before you go home, there's going to be riots here. I think you've jumped out of the frying pan and into the fire, my friend."

"So, are you part of this movement?" I said.

"Heck, yeah," Eddie said, standing and kicking at a rock. "It makes me really mad to hear people talk about 'negro' this and 'negro' that, and say things about how they're all worthless. You remember my friend, Charles?"

I nodded. Charles was about a year older than us, a really smart kid with a great sense of humor. I pictured his smiling face and remembered some of the jokes he'd told me last time I'd seen him. Eddie and Charles were friends, but it was a difficult friendship, mostly because of the townspeople. Charles was black. "Is he okay?" I asked, worried. I knew what had happened to the Freedom Riders, and I knew there had been bombings. Suddenly I was scared for Charles.

Eddie clenched his fists. "No, he got his nose broken when a couple of guys jumped him and pushed him down. Apparently he'd been walking on the wrong part of the sidewalk one afternoon."

"Are we the only ones around here that don't think that kind of thing makes any sense?" I asked.

"We're not the only ones," Eddie said. "My parents, your parents, your grandparents… we all think the same thing, that segregation is wrong. It's time to take a stand."

"It's worse than you think," I said. "Wait 'til you hear about sleazy Al and his cronies." I told Eddie about the group Al had mentioned to us, the men in power that were set on eliminating the negro.

Eddie shuddered. "Are they going to kill people?"

"I don't know, but I wouldn't put it past them. They're not nice people."

Eddie grabbed my arm. "You've gotta come with me and my sister on Friday night. We're going to sneak into a meeting of the Danville Christian Progressive Association."

"Who are they?"

"They're mostly black folks who are meeting to talk about desegregation. My sister and I want to see what they're planning, see if we can help. We've been listening to Martin Luther King, Jr. and we think he's right. Maybe we can be part of a protest, let others know how we feel."

I nodded. "Okay, but what about your parents? Do they know what you're doing?"

"No, my sister and I decided to keep them out of this. They'd probably tell us to stay out of it. They're worried we're going to get hurt." Eddie put his hand out, as if he were going to shake hands with me. "Are you in?"

I took his hand in a solemn handshake. "I'm in."

Nate

I listened to the evening news with a growing sense of dread. I'd sent my son away to keep him safe, but inadvertently sent him into a war zone. I knew that Birmingham and Montgomery were dangerous places, places of riots and bombings.

I never dreamed Danville would come to that as well.

So far we'd gotten one letter from Quinn, which he must have written the day he got to his grandparents.

Dear Mom and Dad,

I'm doing fine, and I got here okay, so don't worry about me. Gram and gramps are great, and it's always fun to be here. Grandpa said we could go fishing, and that maybe he would teach me to use a slingshot as long as I only used it on cans. He said it's not fair to use it on birds and squirrels, as I might hurt them real bad and then they'd have no way to heal.

I don't want you to worry, but Danville is kind of weird right now. There's some people organizing against segregation, and others fixing to keep segregation. I guess it's like that all over the country, though, right?

Me and Eddie and his sister are going to spend some time with a nice Christian group, so I don't want you to worry about me.

I hope you are both well and Mr. Portwell is leaving you alone. I'm sorry to say this, but he's a big, fat worm anus. He'll never get away with whatever he has planned, so don't worry about him.

Grandma says to tell you hello and that she loves you. She'll call you on Sunday when the rates are cheaper.

Love,

Quinn

Maggie leaned over the back of my chair, looking at Quinn's letter that was in my hands. "Our son is a lot like his parents," she said.

"I know," I answered. "As anxious as I am for his safety, I'm proud of him."

We were interrupted by the ringing of the phone, which Maggie went to answer in the kitchen. A few minutes later she returned, her face ashen.

A bolt of fear shot through me. "What happened?"

"That was my mother," she said.

"But it's Tuesday. She never calls on a Tuesday. What's wrong?" Not Quinn. Please, let him be safe.

"You need to go down to Danville and get my parents and Quinn, bring them back here. She said my father and Quinn were arrested."

"What?" I sputtered.

"Those riots they mentioned on the news tonight, the ones where all those high school students had the hoses turned on them?" she asked.

I nodded. I knew that the police had turned the fire hoses on about sixty high school students that had protested inequality. Once they turned the hoses off, the police took out their night sticks, beat the students and dragged them off to jail.

"Quinn?" I whispered. "He was in that group, wasn't he?"

Maggie's eyes filled with tears. "Yes, but he's okay. The problem is, when my father went to get Quinn out of jail, they arrested him too."

"They arrested your father? That's ridiculous. What are the charges?"

"They said it was for contributing to the delinquency of a minor," she said.

I stood. "That does it. I don't know what this country is coming to, but this has got to end. What is wrong with people? Why do the police have to turn hoses on children, or beat them? Our children are not a danger to society; in this case it's the powers-that-be that are the hazard."

Maggie looked me in the eye. "Powers like Al."

"That's right, exactly like Al," I said. "I'm going to leave tonight. I'll take the car so I can get there quicker, then I'm bringing Quinn and your parents back here. There's safety in numbers, Maggie, and we're going to fight this together. No matter what."

Maggie stood and wrapped her arms around me. "Be careful."

"You've got to come with me," I said. "I can't leave you alone."

"Nate, it won't take you that long. Besides, you know that with all the stuff Quinn has and all the stuff my parents have there won't be enough room in the car for me. I'll be fine, just go. Leave now so you can hurry home."

It took me about three and one half hours to drive down US 360 to get to Danville. It was almost ten o'clock at night when I got there. Maggie's mother had left an outside light on over the porch, and I could see her shadow in the front living room window.

I knocked, knowing she'd seen the lights of the car in the driveway.

"Nate, thank God you're here," she said, answering the door. My mother-in-law is a lovely woman, short with a sweet, round face and long curly hair that she normally wore pinned up. Her usual bright smile was replaced by a concerned frown, and there were dark circles under her eyes.

"Where's the jail?" I asked, not even bothering to step inside.

"Let me get my bag, I'm coming with you," she said. I was not going to argue with her, as my mother-in-law, despite her sweet, easygoing demeanor, was sometimes a force to be reckoned with.

Bustling outside, she was pulling on a pair of gloves as she continued to talk. "I wanted to march right down there and get the boys as soon as I heard, but I knew it would be better to wait for you, since you're a lawyer. I didn't want to make things worse than they already are."

We drove to the police station in silence, with Peg pointing at the places I needed to turn. It only took a few minutes to get there.

I steeled myself for a confrontation, but once I announced who I was who I represented, Quinn and my father-in-law were released in under an hour. Although I had a surge of white hot fury at these so-called protectors of the law, I managed to maintain self-control. Barely.

That self-control almost went away as we were walking out the door. After filling out the forms and gathering my family, we all turned to leave. "Hey kid, one more thing," the sergeant at the desk called out. "Try to stay out of things that aren't your business. There's a reason we have the laws we have, and they're for your own good. You cannot mingle with the other races, kid, it only leads to trouble."

Anger bubbled over. "Do. Not. Speak. To. My. Son."

We turned and left.

Making a quick stop at the house, we picked up the suitcases Peg had packed earlier, and got back in the car.

"Dad, what about Eddie?" Quinn asked before we pulled out of the driveway. "Does he have to stay here? It's not safe for him, either."

"We'll see how things go back home, son, but for now it's best for Eddie to stay here. Maybe later this summer he can come for a visit."

"You should've heard his mother," Quinn said. "When she got to the jail, you could hear her yelling all over the building."

Donald chuckled. "It's true. That woman is a force to be reckoned with."

"Why didn't they arrest her?" I asked.

From the corner of my eye I could see Donald shrug. "I don't rightly know," he answered.

"I do," Quinn said. "Eddie told me his mother had some sort of dirt on the chief of police, so he knew if he got arrested they would let him go or else his mother would tell the whole town what she knew."

Peg snorted. "Whatever it is, I'll bet it's good."

Quinn nodded. "That's right, Grandma. It's –"

"Don't tell anyone, Quinn," Donald interrupted. "If you know something like that, keep it to yourself."

"Why?" Quinn asked.

"You might need it," Donald said. "In case you end up back in the Danville jail."

"Don't worry, Grandpa, I'm pretty sure that's not going to happen," Quinn said.

"It might, but you might be doing what your father did tonight," Donald answered.

"What do you mean?"

Donald sighed. "I mean, getting me out of jail."

Maggie

The night I waited for my family to come home from Danville was a very long night. It had been pouring rain for days, and it felt like it would never end. I had an eerie feeling that this was the first of many nights I would be standing at the front window, watching for my loved ones to come home.

Nate and I decided it would be best for my parents to stay here with Quinn and us. Who could have predicted the events in tiny little Danville that would culminate in my son getting thrown in jail? At eleven years old, he'd already seen and heard enough to thrust him into adulthood.

Thoughts of prison made me shudder, causing a sweat to break out along the back of my neck. I didn't know why, but I'd often dreamt of being locked away, cut off from everyone I loved and unable to escape. I rolled the amulet between my thumb and forefinger. "Please," I prayed, "protect me and my family."

It was only a dream, and I knew that would never happen. But now, in light of what this country is going through, I get the feeling that everything I thought I knew is about to change. I wasn't sure what the change would bring, but for the first time in a long time I experienced fear. Fear for my son, my husband, my parents, and yes, fear for my country.

When they finally straggled through the door, wet from the dash to the door and exhausted from their travails, I tried not to show my relief at having them all home.

"Nate will bring your bags upstairs, Mom. Come in, I made some food if you're hungry," I said, hugging my parents and squeezing my son.

"Grandma did this to me when I got to Danville," Quinn squirmed, making everyone laugh.

"Why don't you go on up to bed, son, and get a good night's rest. We'll talk in the morning," I said, giving him one last hug before bed.

Nate, my parents and I filed into the kitchen, the place where we could sit and talk quietly. I don't think any of us really wanted to go to sleep just yet.

My mother put her hands over mine. "I'm so sorry, Maggie, I never meant for this to happen."

"Mom, you can't predict that people will be assholes."

"Margaret Elizabeth," my mother began, then stopped. "You're right, there is no predicting that. Now, let's talk about what we're going to do about your situation with Al. Surely you don't think he's all that dangerous, do you?"

"I think once the election is over we'll be fine," I said. "But that's not until November. It's only June right now. So we have a few months where we have to watch ourselves, and after that we'll see what happens."

"What happens if Al doesn't win?" my father said. "Do you think he'll be dangerous?"

"I think he'll be dangerous if he does win," Nate said. "The problem is, and excuse me for saying it like this, but Al's always been a bullshit artist. I have no idea if what he said about a secret organization is true or not."

The sound of the rain pounding against the windows was all that could be heard, as everyone thought about what it meant if this type of organization did exist.

"Do you really think he would make something like that up?" Peg said.

I shook my head. "No, I don't think so. I think he assumed Nate and I would go along with his little plan, because their friendship goes back to childhood. The thing is, I'm not sure we ever really discussed our political views with Al before, so he must have assumed we were as narrow-minded as he is."

"Who do you think is in this so-called club, if it exists?" Donald asked.

"Nate and I have talked about this a lot," I said. "It's probably people Al knows, people from prominent families, maybe people in law enforcement…"

"I think we've seen that we cannot trust the system right now," Nate said. "As much as it pains me to admit this, there are so many police officers here in the South that are forced to uphold laws that are unfair."

"Do you think Kathy and Mitchell have anything to do with this?" Peg asked.

Nate and I both spoke at the same time. "No," we said.

"Is that what you know to be true, or is that what you want?" Donald asked gently.

"If it were true, I'd know," Nate said. "I've spoken to my sister, asked her a few questions about Al. Apparently, when he stopped by to talk to them Mitchell wasn't home and Kathy wanted to get Al out of the house. When he told her he was running for Senate, she said congratulations and that she fully supported him."

"She was trying to get him to leave," I explained. "I don't blame her; I might have done the same thing. It's really creepy having him come in when I'm alone in the house, I never know what he's going to do."

"For now, I think we should stick to the plan Maggie and I have had, except we'll expand it," Nate said. "Nobody goes anywhere alone. If you have to go out, let the others know where you'll be. If we stay together, the chances of having something happen go down."

I turned to my father. "How long do you think you'll want to stay? Do you have to go back?"

He shrugged. "We've closed the house up for now, and I've got some savings that I put aside. I got fired from my job, anyway, so it doesn't matter. I'm too old to go out and get a new job right now. We'll stay with you as long as you need us."

I was appalled. "What did you get fired for?"

My father smiled at me, the first genuine smile I'd seen since they arrived. "Unseemly conduct. A bunch of people got fired over this thing, Maggie. It doesn't matter. We've got to do what's right, that's the important thing."

"Promise me you'll agree to the plan I outlined," Nate said. "I want to make sure everyone stays safe, since we don't really know what we're facing. Al Portwell comes from power and money, a combination that can be deadly."

Everyone nodded their assent, but as I sat at the kitchen table with my parents a wave of panic rolled over me. It felt like I'd been in this situation before, and the walls were closing in.

I felt like I was fighting a battle I might not have a chance in hell of winning, and my entire family was at stake.

Quinn

My father's plan was a good idea, but it wasn't enough. Al got me anyway.

I realize now that I shouldn't have gone, but it didn't occur to me that I'd be in any danger. I thought there would be lots of people at the Mill, so I left a note for my parents on the kitchen table and left.

Because the rains had been so heavy there was lots of storm damage. The biggest thing that happened, though, was a few days ago when the Waller Mill dam broke, flooding the houses and streets in the area. I'd heard from other people that there was interesting stuff turning up in the debris, and I wanted to go over there and see what was floating around. I also thought maybe I could help anyone that needed clean-up help.

Al must have had guys watching the house, because as soon as I walked out the door and got on my bike someone came up behind me, slapped a hand over my mouth and dragged me into a car. I struggled and tried to kick, but with that darn hand over my mouth I couldn't scream or anything, and whoever grabbed me was big. And strong, very strong. I hated the feeling of being held down. I tried to hold on to being mad about the whole thing, because underneath that I was just plain scared.

My only chance for survival was to come up with a good plan, something that would outsmart Al. I couldn't panic, and I had to pay attention to everything around me so I could tell everyone later what I'd seen.

First, I was shoved into the backseat of an Oldsmobile, pushed onto the seat where I could see clumps of dirt and greasy tools on the floor below me.

I could hear the squeal of tires as the driver sped away. The guy that had grabbed me kept his arm clamped over my mouth, holding me down and keeping me quiet.

I got a good long look at those two guys, which made me nervous.

They don't care if I see them, they're going to kill me. Think, think hard. You're smarter than them, you've got to be.

Nobody said a word for the entire ride, which didn't last long. I knew where we were going even before the car started making turns, and I was not surprised when we reached the old farmhouse that I knew Al liked to use for his 'meetings'. Where else would he take me?

I was shoved out of the car, but the big guy didn't clamp his hand over my mouth again. He didn't have to, nobody was around to hear me scream.

The driver, who I assumed was the leader of the two goons, led us around the back and opened a screen door that led into a kitchen. Al was sitting at a table, sharpening knives and waiting for me.

I flopped into the nearest chair, looked Al in the eye and said, "Thank you. It's about time you came and got me."

Al put his knife back on the table, letting the room remain silent. I waited. Finally, he said, "Why did you want me to come get you?"

I took a deep breath. "I know what you're doing. I've been here before, you know. I know all about your club and your plans."

He leaned forward in his chair and wiped a fleck of spittle from the corner of his mouth. "What do you know, or rather, what do you think you know?"

"I know you're going to get rid of all the niggers," I said, trying to keep a straight face. "And I want to help."

Maggie

When I heard the kitchen door slam, I bolted upright in bed. The morning sunlight was shining directly in my eyes, giving me a headache. But there was more. My instincts as a mother told me my son was in trouble. "Quinn," I screamed, grabbing my robe and running downstairs. On the kitchen table there was a note from Quinn, saying he'd gone to check out the damage from the flood over at the Waller Mill dam, but I knew he wouldn't be there.

"What's wrong?" Nate stumbled into the room, bleary eyed from another sleepless night.

"Quinn, he –" Instead of finishing my sentence, I waved the note at him and ran out the door. When I came back in, Nate was standing in the same spot, holding the note.

"Did you see him?" he asked.

I tried to keep the fear out of my voice. "His bike is sitting in the front yard."

"Get dressed, let's go," Nate said. My mother came into the kitchen, and I filled her in as quickly as I could on what had happened.

"Go," she said. "We'll wait here in case he comes back."

Nate and I drove up and down the streets we knew he'd have to travel to get over to Waller Mill, but of course we didn't find him. I knew, with mounting dread, that Al had my baby.

"We've got to find Al," I said, after driving for what seemed like hours.

Nate put a hand over mine and squeezed. My entire body was frozen, suspended in a state of shock. "Let's go home first and make sure he's not there," he said. "We can grab a bite to eat before heading out again." He looked over at me and I could see the worry carved onto his face. "We may be in for a long day," he said.

When we got back to the house, my mother met us at the door. She didn't ask, just held the door open for us and steered me toward the kitchen table. She'd made pancakes and had them waiting on the table, but I couldn't eat. Everything tasted dry, and I felt like choking every time I swallowed.

My son was out there, somewhere, with that monster.

I could hear Nate in the other room on the phone, and after a minute he came back in. "I called Mitchell," he said. "He's on his way over, and told me not to worry. He said kids do stuff like this all the time."

"You didn't tell him about Al?" Peg asked.

A horrifying thought occurred to me. "What if he's in on it?"

Nate looked at me, confused. "What? Do you mean Mitchell?"

I nodded, not caring that tears were pouring down my face. "Remember Al told us that he had Mitchell and Kathy's support? What if they really are part of this whole thing? What if he won't help us?"

Donald came and sat next to me, my kind and loving father who was always there when I needed him. "Baby, you've got to pull yourself together. I know after what happened this summer down in Danville it's kind of hard to trust the police, but right now you don't have much choice. Besides, Mitchell is the boy's uncle, he's not going to want to see anything bad happen to him."

I took a breath, willing myself to remain calm. "You're right, Dad, I just can't seem to stop all these terrible thoughts from going through my head."

"I know, baby, but you've got to stay strong. Do it for Quinn," Donald said. There had been a time in my life when my father and I did not get along, when for no apparent reason I intensely disliked him. As far as I knew he'd never done anything to warrant that kind of reaction from me, it was more of an instinctual response on my part.

I never understood it, since my father spent much of his time doting on me and making sure I knew I was loved and cared for. Finally, as an adult, I realized what a good man my father was, and I let go of my odd anger and let him into my heart. On this particular morning, I was grateful he was with us. My father is a strong and steadfast character, and I knew that whatever lay ahead for us he would do his part to ensure Quinn came home safely.

It was a good half hour before Mitchell showed up at our house. Nate let him in, and I could hear the hum of their voices coming from the living room. At this point my heart hurt from pounding so hard in my chest, and I felt a frantic sense of despair at the thought of Quinn out there on his own.

"Good morning, Maggie," Mitchell said as he strode into the room. "Tell me what's going on here."

Standing in front of me he listened carefully as I told him everything I knew, from Al's threats to the disappearance of Quinn.

Pulling out a chair and sitting at the table, Mitchell asked, "You say the boy left a note? Can I see it?"

I pulled the slightly crumpled note out of my skirt pocket and handed it to him. "See, it says here that he went to Waller Mill, but he's not there. Mitchell, you've got to alert everyone. This is serious."

Mitchell looked at the note for a full minute before answering. When he did, I knew he was having trouble saying what he had to say. "Maggie, listen to me carefully. I know that you and Kathy don't like Al all that much, and I know that sometimes he can be a bit pushy. But it's a long way from flirting with you to kidnapping a boy."

I started to protest, but Mitchell held up a hand. "Hear me out, Maggie, just hear me out. The thing is, Quinn left you a note. Just because he isn't where he said he was going doesn't me he's been kidnapped. There's no evidence of that."

"But his bike is still here," I cried. "Where would he go without his bike?"

"Is there any sign of a struggle? Any blood in your house or yard?" Mitchell asked. When both Nate and I shook our heads, Mitchell sighed. "I'm sorry, but legally there's nothing I can do. Once he's been missing for a little bit longer I'll file a report."

"Why do we have to wait? He's missing right now," I said, frustrated by Mitchell's apparent lack of interest.

"Maggie, kids do stuff like this all the time. You have no idea the stuff I see every day, the stuff that people do to each other. This is a typical kid prank, and Quinn will be back home by dinner, don't you worry." Mitchell stood to leave, and nodded at Nate. "Call me as soon as you hear anything."

"Mitchell, I understand the kinds of things you see on patrol, but remember, I see those same things in the courtroom," Nate said. "And I'm telling you, Quinn would not pull a prank like this. That's the main reason we sent him down to Danville, to try to keep him safe."

Mitchell looked thoughtful. "Yeah, I heard ya'll got yourselves in a bit of a mess down there. Sorry to hear about that."

I wanted to strangle him, regardless of the fact that he had a gun. My son was in danger, and this idiot police officer wasn't going to help us.

I jumped to me feet and took a step toward Mitchell. "Not only are you wrong, but if anything happens to my son I am personally coming after you, Mitchell."

He took a step backward. "You can't threaten a police officer, Maggie."

"You're sworn to uphold the law, and you're not doing anything as far as I can see. That's a crime," I said. "You're his uncle, I expected more from you. So either get your sorry self out there and find my son or get the hell out of my way." I stomped past him and went upstairs to pull myself together and come up with a new plan.

I needed to save Quinn.

Nate

It was all my fault. I should have been more strict with Quinn about the rules of staying safe. I should have forbidden him to go anywhere alone. I should have never been friends with Al. I should have punched Al in the face when I'd had the chance. I shouldn't have been such an idiot about human nature.

But I couldn't focus on any of those things, since I had to find my son before it was too late. The sharp sound of knocking at the front door took me by surprise.

Before I had the door fully open, I knew who would be standing on my front step. "Al," I said. "Come in." I followed my former friend into the front room, reminding myself that if I killed him now I might never find my son.

"What do you want?" My words were coated in ice, but I didn't care. I was beyond game playing.

Maggie materialized by my side, and I grabbed her hand. Al glanced at that and smiled. "That's so sweet," he said. "You two always did have the hots for each other, even in college."

Neither Maggie nor I spoke, waiting to see what Al would say. Walking around the front room, Al acted as if he were looking at our things for the first time.

Finally, Al said, "I was wondering if you'd had a chance to think about our recent conversation."

"What about it?" I asked, aware that I had to tread carefully. As much as I wanted to rip into him, I needed to help Quinn.

"I really was hoping for your support, you know," Al continued. "I think once you've had time to think about it, maybe discuss it with your family, you'll start to understand more about my goals."

"Discuss it with our family?" Maggie asked, her voice dangerously high. I squeezed her hand again, willing her not to tear into Al.

Al smiled. "Yes, your family. You should talk to your lovely son, and even your mother, Nate. As I've said before, she is a remarkable woman."

"You want us to talk about your plans with our son and my mother," I repeated, waiting for his next move. There was no doubt in my mind that this was a game to Al, but I had no idea how far he was willing to take it.

"Yes," Al answered, crossing his arms over his chest. "I think that if you listen to reason and try to fully understand what's at stake here then everything will work out fine. We all have a lot to lose, don't we?"

There was a moment of silence before I asked the question that had been plaguing me for days. "Why did you tell me about this, Al? You know what kind of person I am, what made you think I would agree with you on this issue?"

Al gave a small bark of a laugh before answering. "If you want to know the truth, it's because your mother insisted on it." I was caught off balance, and my face must have shown my surprise, because he laughed again. "Your mother has been supporting my projects for years, just as I've been supporting hers. Didn't you know that?"

I shook my head, feeling nauseous. I couldn't think about the fact that my mother was involved now, I'd have to save that piece of information for later.

Al walked closer to me and extended his hand as if for a handshake. "So, are we in agreement?" he asked.

I hesitated, then took his hand and shook it. "Yes. Yes we are."

Quinn

I think Al believed me when I complained about my parents, and he even laughed when I went on and on about them and their liberal horse-puckey ideas of how things should be. It took a while, but I talked and talked as if I'd been waiting for a friend to unload all my feelings. I acted like Al was my savior, and practically begged him to adopt me.

I hated doing it, but it was the only way I could think of to give my parents time to find me. I knew they would, but I had to stay alive long enough for them to get me.

The other possibility, which blossomed in my mind last night, was that I could escape. Because with the recent turn of events, it looked like I was going to have to take more action than I first thought.

Understandably, Al was doubtful at first. But my time in the Danville jail had been well spent, because I'd listened to both sides and picked up some of their expressions. I used words like 'worthless' and 'segregation' enthusiastically, then I praised Senator Byrd for all I was worth. Senator Byrd, who had once been governor of Virginia, was a big promoter of the 'Southern Manifesto', a vile piece which denounced the Supreme Court's order to desegregate.

I did my best to sound convincing, even though at times I choked on my words.

I think Al finally decided I was telling the truth, because he started to open up to me and tell me his plans. That was both a good and bad thing.

It was good because I was pretty certain it meant he wasn't going to kill me. It was bad because he told me about the man he was going to kill, a colored man living on the outskirts of Williamsburg.

He might have already had this murder planned, but I think that he told me about it to test me, see what I would say. I tried to stay enthusiastic, even telling him I would help with the murder.

That was the hardest thing I've ever done in my life, saying those words, but I knew that if I didn't there would be two dead people in Williamsburg.

"Are you going to shoot him?" I asked Al. "Or are we going to beat him?"

Al laughed. "Neither, boy. We're going to use a little trick I learned from your grandmother. She's a very smart lady, you know. Maybe when this is all over you can go live with her. I'm sure she'd be happy to have you; it would make up for your father not turning out the way she'd planned."

I couldn't stop the words from tumbling out of my mouth. "Grandma knows how to kill people?"

"She's been doing it for years, although the first time it didn't work out so well," Al said. "But it's not like she does the actual killing, she just sends people in with instructions on what to do."

"What are we going to do?"

"We're going to set fire to the house that colored boy lives in. We're going to burn him alive."

Maggie

The only thing that had stopped me from putting my hands around Al's throat when he stopped by earlier was the fact that it would make things worse for Quinn, wherever he was. I was upstairs in my room, trying to rest but too anxious to do anything but stare at the ceiling. Nate had gone to his office, saying he was going to look into Al's background and that he would be back soon.

I hated feeling so useless, but I didn't know what to do at that point. I thought about walking the streets and looking for Quinn, but dismissed the idea. I knew it was pointless.

I heard the downstairs door slam, and Nate's voice yelling up to me. "Maggie!"

I ran out of the room and down the stairs, hoping Nate had brought Quinn home. "Do you have him?"

"No," Nate said. "But I think I know where he is. Let's go." He grabbed my hand and started pulling me.

When we got into the car, Nate started talking. "I had this idea that Al must have brought Quinn somewhere, but it had to be a place where nobody would notice. So I went down to City Hall and started searching through the records. Sure enough, Al owns property that he never talked about."

"What? Where is it?"

"It's over on Strawberry Plains Road. It's a small bungalow. I've been there before, he told me he uses it as a sort of retreat."

"Retreat from what?"

Nate shrugged. "I don't know, but I'm guessing he used this place as a spot for his meetings. He probably wasn't ready to tell me about it."

I knew I had to say something, and now was as good a time as any. "Nate, about your mother –"

He held up a hand to stop me. "Don't. Just don't. I can't even think about that right now. I'm going to have to deal with it eventually, but right now it's that one thing too many for me to process."

I nodded. I could certainly understand that. "I just want you to know that I'm here for you," I said.

He looked at me and smiled a small, tight smile. "I've never doubted that for one second. I wish everyone were as fine and supportive as you, Maggie."

We drove for a few more minutes in silence, then Nate pulled the car off to the side of the road.

"What are we doing?" I asked. "Where's the house?"

"We can park and walk from here. I don't want them to know we're coming, we've got a better chance of saving Quinn if we can sneak in."

We moved quickly, trying to stay low as we ran through other yards and dashed from one spot to another. I couldn't quite catch my breath, especially as thoughts of my son raced through my head.

After a few minutes Nate put a finger to his lips and pointed to a small house. It was weather-beaten, a shotgun shack with a small front porch. There were no cars in the driveway, but I knew better than to assume nobody was there. I didn't think I'd ever be able to assume anything or trust anyone again.

After we ran to the back of the house, we tried to look in the windows. There were a few pieces of furniture scattered around the room, but we didn't see any live occupants. My eye fixated on one object, though, tucked into the corner of the room. It was my amulet, the one given to me by my aunt.

"He was here," I whispered. "Look, it's my amulet. I gave it to him to wear last night, for luck. Do you think he's still in there?"

Nate looked at me. "Let's go find out."

The back door was open, not a surprise in a town like Williamsburg. Nobody locked their door, as nobody expected any real crime. Especially the criminals.

The house was small, one floor with a living room, kitchen, three bedrooms and a bathroom. That was it. Nobody was there, but it was clear from the detritus left behind that people had been there recently. Including Quinn.

I scooped the amulet off the floor and put it around my neck. "I swear, Nate, this thing saved my life once, I know it will save us again."

Nate grabbed my hand. "Let's go, we've got to get out of here and figure out where he is. I don't like that he's not here."

We started walking back toward the car, not bothering to hide as we'd done on our way in since there was no one to see us. I couldn't help it, the weight of despair settled around me like a millstone. Tears flowed freely down my face, but I didn't care. All that mattered was getting my son back.

"We'll find him," Nate said. "We just have to think for a minute, figure out where he could have gone."

"You mean where Al could have taken him," I said.

As we walked, I became aware of a car following behind us, slowly. I grabbed Nate's arm and turned around. It was Mitchell, and he pulled the police cruiser onto the side of the road behind us.

"I thought that was you two," he said, getting out of the car. "What are you doing out here, walking down the road?"

I hesitated. I'd known Mitchell for years, he'd been to our house a number of times, and I never had any reason to believe he was anything but an honest man doing his job. He was my brother-in-law, and I wanted to believe in him. Mitchell never gave me the creeps like Al had, because he'd never done anything that wasn't completely above-board.

I needed his help, and I needed to trust him. "Quinn was here," I said.

"What do you mean, Quinn was here?" Mitchell asked.

I looked at Nate, who looked back at me. I knew my husband was thinking the same thing I was, and I knew it was time to put our faith in Mitchell. I just hoped he wouldn't let us down.

"Remember we told you that Al was behind Quinn's disappearance?" I didn't wait for Mitchell to respond before continuing with my story. "We have proof now. Nate found out that Al owns this house, and Quinn was here, but now he's gone again. We have to find him before Al does something truly horrible. I think he's going to kill my son." Those last words escaped out on a sob, and Mitchell came and put a hand on my shoulder, leading both of us over to his car.

"Okay, I want both of you to get in the car right now and tell me everything that's happened since I last saw you," he said.

I got in the front seat and Nate got in the back seat, with Mitchell behind the wheel. Nate leaned forward and told Mitchell everything we knew, including the part about Al's visit as well as his comment about Nate's mother.

Mitchell ran a hand over his face, looking more tired than I'd ever seen him. "Damn," he said. "I really hoped that wasn't true."

"What are you talking about, Mitchell?" Nate asked.

Mitchell hesitated for a fraction of a second, then apparently decided it was time to talk. "There have been rumors through the years, but that's all they've been were rumors. I'd heard from a few sources that your mother was the person responsible for setting that fire."

"Fire?" I asked, confused. I was having trouble making the connection between a fire and my son's disappearance.

"The fire in your aunt's back yard," Mitchell clarified.

"The one that could have killed you," Nate whispered. "Why?"

I knew right then exactly why. Alice Kay was a smart woman, and observant as well. She'd seen my bouts of morning sickness and even commented on my tiredness. "She knew I was pregnant," I said.

Nate let out a haunted sound, a strangled cry that broke my heart. "Will you please help us find my son?" he said to Mitchell, pulling himself together with a visible effort.

Mitchell nodded. "It's not that I didn't believe you, I just needed to be sure. But after what you've told me…" He shook his head. "I'm calling it in right now. Don't worry, I'll put out an all-points-bulletin for both Quinn and Al."

Reaching for his radio, Mitchell spoke into the handset, saying the magic code words that would alert the entire police community about our son. When he finished, he looked at us. "I'm sorry it's come to this, and I'm sorry I didn't listen to you sooner. Now, let's put our heads together and drive through town. I want you both to stay with me, at least I can keep the two of you safe."

He put the car in gear and pulled out onto the road. For a minute, there was only silence, broken only by the sound of static coming from the radio.

"Where are we going?" I asked.

Mitchell's face was grim. "If what you say is true and Al is behind this, then I have a feeling he's looking to start trouble. Let's head east over by Route 60 and see what we can find."

"Why east? What's over there?" I said.

"The community of Grove," Mitchell said.

"That's a predominantly negro community," Nate said. "Why do you think Quinn is there?"

"Because I think Al is going to start trouble," Mitchell said. "And I'd like to stay one step ahead of him this time."

Quinn

I knew I didn't have much time, but I had to get over to the Grove. That was the section of town where the negroes lived, and I knew that's where Al and his cronies were headed. I waited until I was certain nobody was in the house, pretending to be asleep. I'd gained Al's trust today, especially since we talked about all those things he held dear. I think I was pretty convincing, letting him know how much I hated everything my parents stood for, and how much I admired him.

Of course, it was all a lie. I didn't know what else to do, so I pretended to be relieved that Al had come and gotten me. Before I snuck out I took off the necklace mom gave me last night and dropped it on the floor, a signal to my parents that I'd been in the house. I hope they find it.

Martin Luther King, Jr. Bayard Rustin. I could hear their voices in my head, talking about standing up for what was right, but doing it in a non-violent way. Today I had to face men who wanted to kill, people who wanted to hurt others for no reason other than the fact that hatred burned in their hearts. I had to save a man from death, and save myself at the same time.

I wouldn't let myself get scared, because I knew as soon as I let the fear take over I wouldn't be able to keep going.

Al was very clear. There was a man who lived over in the Grove section that had to die, and he had to die today. Al told me that this guy, Horatio Jackson, was uppity. He'd insulted Al by talking back, daring to express an opinion when he should've kept his mouth shut. If there was one thing Al didn't like, it was people that went against him. Al was going to teach this man a lesson, teach the whole negro community a lesson.

Al said that people like that had to be put in their place, they had to be shown that they were worthless, they weren't even people. I think Al was a little bit afraid of this guy, because he said that Horatio was trying to organize people in Williamsburg to head up to Washington this summer. There's going to be something called a March on Washington for Jobs and Freedom, and it's all about civil rights. Horatio was signing people up for the bus, and Al found out about it. Al said Horatio has caused trouble before, and it's obvious something has to be done.

I say good for Horatio, but of course I didn't say it out loud. As soon as Al started telling me the story of how they were going to teach Horatio a lesson, I knew

I had to do something. I also knew that this was going to be the fight of, and for, my life.

I wasn't sure exactly where I was going, I only knew Al had told me that they were going to kill a man in the Grove. I think he believed everything I told him, but I'm sure Al still thought of me as just a kid. After all, kids are invisible, they don't really count as people. What difference did one boy make in the grand scheme of things?

I kept off the main road and made my way through back yards, trying to keep myself as invisible as possible. I knew people might see me, but again, because I'm a kid I knew most folks wouldn't pay any attention to me.

My breath was coming in short, ragged gasps, and the hot June air burned my lungs. My legs weren't moving fast enough and I knew time was running out. I was on foot, but I was certain that Al's guys were driving that Oldsmobile as fast as they could.

Finally, I did something I never thought I'd do. I saw a bicycle leaning against a front porch, and I grabbed it. I didn't have time to think about right and wrong, I needed to move faster.

I couldn't let someone die because of me. The problem was, I had no idea what I was going to do once I got there.

How will I find the right house? What am I going to do once I find the house? How can I save someone and not get myself killed?

I knew one thing, no matter what I had to see this thing through. No matter what.

Maggie

I heard the radio squawk as we headed east, and I saw a shadow cross Mitchell's face. I didn't understand what the codes meant, but I knew it had to do with us. All I heard was the address. 138 Howard Drive.

Mitchell pressed on the accelerator, his face grim.

"Isn't that a church?" I asked. Mitchell nodded.

"There's some sort of disturbance going on there," he said. "I'm pretty sure we've found our trouble. Hang on, here we go. When we get there, I need for both of you to stay in the car, do you understand?"

Neither Nate nor I answered. I didn't know what to say, because if my son was in trouble in that church nothing would keep me out of there. I'm pretty sure Nate felt the same way. After a moment, Mitchell blew out an exasperated breath. "Listen, I can't be worried about either of you getting hurt in there. I need to be able to focus on taking care of what's going on, and saving Quinn. Do I have your word you'll stay out of the way?"

"We'll do our best," Nate said. "But if push comes to shove, and I think I'm the only one who can save my boy, you can't stop me."

Mitchell nodded. "That's about what I expected."

"What's happening?" I asked, knowing that those codes that came over the radio meant something.

Mitchell didn't answer, and focused instead on driving. His silence made me more nervous, but I didn't ask again. We'd be there soon enough.

When we pulled into the parking lot I could see a group of people huddled together, fearful looks on their faces. Mitchell was out of the car almost before it stopped moving. When he opened the car door, I could hear crying.

I saw Quinn standing in the midst of the group in the parking lot.

"Quinn!" Mitchell turned and opened the car door for me, letting me out so I could get to my son.

As I ran toward Quinn, a loud whooshing sound came from the church. Looking over, I saw smoke pouring out of the windows.

"Fire!" someone yelled, and people started running.

Above the noise of the fire and the din of the crowd a single voice could be heard, wailing. "My baby's in there, my baby's in there!" A woman was screaming, trying to run into the burning building, but others held her back.

"You can't go in there, you'll get hurt," someone said to her.

"My baby!" she screamed.

That was the moment everything slowed. The noise disappeared, and when I looked over at Quinn I saw him run straight into the building. Nate hesitated long enough for me to force the amulet that had been around my neck into his hands. I watched as he put it in the pocket of his shirt, then raced into the building after Quinn.

The fire was raging now, consuming everything. The sparks flew into the black sky like the fireflies we caught last year. I stood very still, watching the men I loved most in this world go straight into that inferno.

The voice spoke into my ear. I knew that voice, I'd heard it before, but I'd only heard it in my dreams. "Don't fear the fire. They'll be fine, I'll take care of them. They'll come out with the little girl in a moment. He has the necklet."

Looking up at the church I can see her, the woman in my dreams that speaks to me of herbs and medicines. The healer-woman who brings me comfort at night, the one I've never talked about with anyone. Her beautiful black face shines as she smiles at me, and her arms open wide, showing me her cloak made from plants and small flowers. Roots grow into her brown skin, connecting her to the earth.

Everything will be fine. I repeat it over and over again, clinging to nothing but hope. I stand and wait for my boys to come back to me.

I don't know how much time passed, but I could have sworn it was forever before Nate and Quinn stumbled out of the church. Quinn was hanging on to Nate, who carried a small girl in his arms. She looked to be about five years old.

Her mama ran to my husband, sobbing. "Oh dear Lord, thank you, thank you," she cried, taking her daughter into her arms.

My boys smile and walk toward me.

That's when Al charged out of that same door Quinn and Nate had just escaped through. I can see the anger on his face, an anger and hatred he has born in his soul for centuries. Like the fire, his rage is ready to consume anything in its path, and he is headed straight for Quinn.

Above, the woman in the cloak opens her arms wider and I can feel the warmth of her love for all living things.

Mitchell moves between Quinn and Al, standing with his legs slightly apart and his gun drawn. Al says something, I can see his mouth move, and Mitchell pulls the trigger.

I know without having to be told that Al is dead the moment that bullet pierces his heart. I see his soul lifted up into the arms of the healer, surrounded by a shining light, and he is gone.

It is over.

Nate

It is done. I'll never know how we managed to make it out of that church alive, but I'm not going to question a miracle that saved my son and me.

After Al died, I went to see my mother. Mitchell was with me, as I wanted to have a witness. It went the way I expected it would.

She sat in the drawing room, perfectly poised with her back straight.

"Mother, I've learned about some things that have happened, things we need to discuss."

"Nathaniel, I do not like your tone," my mother answered.

"Alice Kay, I do not like the fact that you tried to kill my wife," I replied.

She sniffed. "That woman was never good enough for you. You had an obligation to live up to our family name, and you married beneath you." Turning to Mitchell, she looked him up and down. "Both you and your sister have been such a disappointment."

Mitchell and I walked out of there without another word. I don't expect to see my mother again, unless it's by accident. If anyone asks, I'll tell them I don't have a mother.

I'm going to run for Senate. Maggie, Mitchell and my sister Kathy all convinced me to do this. They may be right, it might be time to try to take a political stand. Virginia certainly needs help, and if what Al had said to me was correct, there are plenty of men out there doing their part to ruin this country. I cannot stand by and watch that happen.

It's a warm September day, and I think we're starting to put the events of the summer behind us. I came home from work early, anxious to see my family. Mitchell had stopped by to check on Maggie. He stopped me in the front yard. "You know, something has been bothering me."

"What?" I asked.

"Well, the night of the fire, I remember Maggie handed you something just before you went into that church that was afire. What was that all about?"

"Oh, she gave me some mumbo-jumbo necklace that her Aunt gave her. You know, the one she wears all the time. That ivory thing."

"Nope – never seen it on her. What's it supposed to do?"

"Oh, it has powers or something. Some sort of voodoo. Anyway, good seeing you. Got to get inside. I've got a trip planned in November. I'm taking them to Dallas to meet Kennedy."

I watched my brother-in-law walk back to his patrol car and get behind the wheel. He didn't start the engine right away. I waved and headed into the house.

"Maggie, Quinn," I called out as I walked into the kitchen. "Come on down, I've got a surprise for you."

Maggie walked into the kitchen, and I could hear the rumble of Quinn's feet on the stairs before he appeared.

"What's the surprise, Dad?" he asked.

I pulled Maggie into my arms, and reached out to touch the top of Quinn's head. "We've had a rough time of it lately, but I think that all things considered we're doing fairly well," I said. "I know it's going to take some time to heal, but I was thinking of taking a little vacation might be good for us."

"That sounds like fun," Quinn said.

"Where do you want to go?" Maggie asked. "It's still warm enough to go to some of the beaches, were you thinking of South Carolina?"

I shook my head, smiling. "No, I was thinking of something a little different. I have it on good authority that our president will be traveling this November, and we've been invited to go down to Dallas to see him."

"Really?" Quinn said, eyes wide. "Do you mean we're going to get to see John F. Kennedy?"

I nodded. "Yes. What do you think; do you want to go to Dallas?"

Maggie hugged me. "I think it would be perfect. It's a great plan, especially with you entering the political arena."

"That was nice of Mitchell to stop by," I said.

"Yes," she answered as she fingered the amulet around her neck. "Listen, I need to run back and check the laundry. You boys get a snack. It will be awhile before dinner is ready."

"Quinn, were you here in the kitchen when Mitchell was talking to you mother?"

"Yes."

"And did she have the necklace on – you know, the amulet?"

"Yes, dad. You know she never takes it off. Well, almost never. Just to save me from stuff. Other than that, she wears it all of the time."

I noticed Mitchell had left his note pad on the counter. I looked out the window and saw his car was still in the driveway.

"Run this out to your uncle." Quinn took the notebook from me and ran out the back door. He was gone for a minute or two, and then came back with a puzzled look on his face.

"That was weird," Quinn said.

"What?"

"Well, Uncle Mitchell was talking to some guy on the radio. The last thing he said before he realized I was there was "November. Dallas. How did he know?"

"I told him before I came in."

Maggie was back, chattering about the trip. I forgot about everything – the amulet, Quinn's comment – everything in the excitement.

And so it was settled. We would travel to Dallas in November, and spend time together as a family healing from the events of the summer.

And whatever the future held for me and my family, I knew we could make it through anything together. We'd been through what felt like lifetimes of the worst, and we survived.

Acknowledgements

First, we'd like to acknowledge our husbands who put up with us waking them up at 2 AM and asking them how long it takes for a body to burn. You know…romantic stuff. Oh, yeah – and they are willing to eat Cheerios for dinner…or fix it themselves. What a great couple of guys were are fortunate enough to be married to.

And our families who support us and read our books and tell us the truth.

And our friends who do the same.

To all the other authors who have researched the time periods in this book. Kudos!

And to the two references here:

1-Way Stations by Elizabeth Robins

2 Barbara Learning, Katherine Hepburn (New York, Crown Publishers, 1995), 274-5

ABOUT THE AUTHORS

JM Johansen lives in Deltaville, Virginia with her husband Carl.

Narielle Living, her husband Steve and their son reside in Yorktown, Virginia.

They have written separately and together. Between the two authors, they have 5 published books:

They teach a seminar on Collaborative Writing called *Two Heads Are Better Than One*.

For more information about the authors and the Chesapeake Bay Karma series please visit their websites

www.NarielleLiving.com
www.JM-Johansen.com
www.HighTidePublications.com

Thanks for reading!